MW00568917

NIGHT WATCH

KEVIN ARMSTRONG

PENGUIN

Published by the Penguin Group

Penguin Books Canada Ltd, 10 Alcorn Avenue, Toronto, Ontario, Canada M4V 3B2

Penguin Books Ltd, 80 Strand, London WC2R 0RL, England

Penguin Putnam Inc., 375 Hudson Street, New York, New York 10014, U.S.A.

Penguin Books Australia Ltd, 250 Camberwell Road, Camberwell, Victoria 3124, Australia

Penguin Books (NZ) Ltd, cnr Rosedale and Airborne Roads, Albany, Auckland 1310, New Zealand

Penguin Books Ltd, Registered Offices: Harmondsworth, Middlesex, England

First published 2002

1 3 5 7 9 10 8 6 4 2

The following stories have appeared previously:
"The Canefield" in *Event* and *13: The Journey Prize Anthology*;
"The First Motion of Love" in *Grain* and *01: Best Canadian Fiction*.

Manufactured in Canada.

NATIONAL LIBRARY OF CANADA CATALOGUING IN PUBLICATION DATA

Armstrong, Kevin, 1973–

ISBN 0-14-100082-1

I. Title.

PS8551.R76374N53 2002 C813'.6 C2002-900186-2
PR9199.4.A75N53 2002

Visit Penguin Canada's website at **www.penguin.ca**

for my father and mother

iv. DEATH BY WATER

Phlebas the Phoenician, a fortnight dead,
Forgot the cry of gulls, and the deep sea swell
And the profit and loss.
A current under sea
Picked his bones in whispers. As he rose and fell
He passed the stages of his age and youth
Entering the whirlpool.
Gentile or Jew
O you who turn the wheel and look to windward,
Consider Phlebas, who was once handsome and tall as you.

—T. S. Eliot, "The Waste Land"

CONTENTS

NIGHT WATCH

NIGHT WATCH

HE WANTS TO TELL IT FROM THE BEGINNING. HE WANTS to leave out nothing from that first night when their cab pulled up to the marina: the way she appeared from behind Curt like something flushed from cover, and how in the back of his mind he knew, knew all along but thought he could take it, wanting to cross this ocean so badly he would have stepped over his mother's burning corpse. His journal tells him little. Thirty days of entries stitch like plots across a marine chart: they show where he was, but say nothing about how. From thirty days of sky and water, only jagged, hate-filled lines like *If things don't improve I just may fuck his wife for him.*

THE BAR WAS EMPTY—just me and the Aussie owner. I was bitching about how things had gone to hell in Tahiti, how my old watering holes were hotels now, or so touristy they hurt my heart just to drink in them, when I noticed their yacht nearing the lagoon. We watched them pick through the reef-lined pass and dump their mainsail before dropping anchor just aft of where my *Soma* was sitting.

"One-week warriors," the Aussie scoffed. "Kite in on bloody jumbos till it's time to piss off home."

I smiled. We both knew he'd go bankrupt without them.

Minutes later I heard a dinghy outboard rev up. The old man steered them in slowly, but when they reached the dock and slipped under the palm-thatched roof it was clear straight away they weren't the sort we'd been expecting.

First off, their skin: a deep-baked brown, from the skipper on down to the kid. And their clothes. Doesn't matter what charterers wear, it always has that brand-new sheen to it, even the ruler folds from the store sometimes. But this trio's gear was faded, worn in.

"Gin and tonic, if you please. The Tanqueray there. Poppet, what will you have?"

"Mmmm, yes, a Tanq and tonic sounds nice. Yes, that would be fine."

Skipper looked in his late fifties, though his hair was still blond. She was shorter, and nearly half as old, with brown hair straight down to the shoulders. Small tits, but her legs were good, face pretty in a bland sort of way.

The kid watched the Aussie pour rum for him, then turned to me.

"That yours out front?"

I nodded.

"Nice lines. What is she, forty feet?"

"Forty-four. Yeah, she's a good ship."

He took a long pull from his drink. "So, you a neurologist or just a Huxley fan?"

"Bit of both, I guess. How's the charter going?"

"Price is right. We just delivered a Bellatrix from San Diego and the company gave us a freebie, their way of saying thanks."

I grimaced out toward their vessel, another Bellatrix. They were one of the most popular charter boats in the world because they were all about compromise: safety for comfort, that is. They had loads of headroom because their decks were dangerously domed, their hulls shallow-veed. Their masts were stepped farther forward to allow for larger dining tables. I'd seen one split on a reef in Tonga: nice teak interior, but the moulding might as well have been Tupperware.

"California's a long haul," I said. "Wouldn't want to weather a storm in one of those."

His eyes flicked to where Skipper and the woman sat, pretending not to listen. "Seemed like a good idea at the time."

HE HAD FOUR DAYS TO FLY to San Diego. He'd been sailing a while, but that doesn't prepare you for crossings. Nothing can, really. With his windburned face and beard, Captain Curt looked like he'd stepped from a Coleridge poem. On land, he seemed a decent enough guy, but there was temper in him like glass shards. And if someone solo-circumnavigates, odds are they go alone for a reason. Leah was younger than him by exactly the kid's age: twenty-three years. Perhaps she was meant to take care of him in his dotage. That, or she was right about the money.

A day before they sailed she threatened to leave.

"But you're *married*. I mean, you can't just jump ship!"

She stared out the window of the small rental car. Under orders, the kid had tried to find her a beach for nearly an hour, without luck. Three complete naval bases, but no beach.

"I don't sleep with Curt much; don't really like to. On our last delivery there was this other woman . . . goodness, I've never met such a . . . *manipulative* person in all my life."

Her tale unfurled like a worn sail. How this *American* had befriended them and come aboard in the Azores. How when the weather warmed she emerged from her cabin all brown and sleek in a bone-white bikini. How she smoothed on lotion until Curt was rabid for her, and Leah invisible. How, when they were at anchor one night, Leah slipped into the water and swam ashore.

"I stayed in a hotel and hung around the docks. Curt didn't have much money; in a week it was gone and she left him, just vanished. He spent another week looking for her before crawling back to me."

"When was this?"

"A month ago. We stayed in St. Thomas to work things out, then were offered this new delivery. But it's different now; I'm afraid. I think he's going to *kill* me."

"What for?"

"The money's all mine. He's tired of me."

The kid gave her a thoughtful look. She might be crazy, might be totally *fucked up*, but they were leaving the next day and needed three bodies on board for the insurance coverage. And lurking sharklike under his surface was the fact that he wanted her aboard. Curt's every move bore a hard-won assurance, but the kid had never met a less introspective man in his life. He could not imagine them lasting alone together. Besides, Leah had a crush on him. That he saw this as interesting, not dangerous, showed how naive he really was. Instead of supporting her mutiny or running himself, he touched her arm and promised to take care of her. They would be friends.

THE KID WAITED AS LONG AS POSSIBLE before introducing us; I guess he knew what was going to happen. Curt had led quite a life: Royal Navy at fifteen, oil rigs in the North Sea, then a solo circumnavigation round Cape Horn in his storm ship *Rover*. Say what you like about imagination, but his limbs looked decades younger than the rest of him. A tough SOB, but with drifting eyes like his woman. You could tell there was something not right there. She stayed quiet at first, but once she got going there was no stopping her.

"John, have you been to St. Thomas? Quite a dodgy place, really. Quite pretty, but really very dodgy, don't you think? There's a lot of crime now, and the water's so dirty in the harbours. But tell me about your passage. It took us thirty days from Shelter Island. Do you know it? America is such an amazing place. We had a hard time after the Tuamotus, though. Hardly any wind at all. And then we had to wait five days in Pap*ee*t*ee* before Customs showed up. Did they give you any problems?"

Finally Skipper let her have it.

"Leah, would you *be quiet!* You don't have to go butting in all the time!"

Her head pulled back, eyes on him sidelong. "I just want to hear his adventures. Surely there's nothing wrong with that, surely. John, you don't mind me asking, do you?"

"Not at all."

Her every statement ended with a question, slim body tensed. I almost invited her back to *Soma* for a smoke to calm her down, then thought better of it. Dockside, the kid leaned over a fenced oceanarium where a green turtle and two black-tip sharks cruised in endless circles.

"So is there a woman waiting for you at home?"

"*Poppet!*"

Right, I thought, *time to go*. The sun looked hung up on some palms near the edge of the lagoon. I drained my glass and stood.

"Nice meeting you both, but dinner's calling."

Leah got up and stepped toward me, a tight look on her face. "We were planning to eat here tonight. Would you care to join us?"

"That's kind, but the gin's pricey enough as it is." I dropped some franc notes on the bar, then felt her hand on my arm.

"My treat; I insist."

Her fingers were thin with short, chewed nails. Their grip was surprisingly firm, and when I looked up, her gaze got me thinking.

We took the table near the water, its lit kerosene lamp like our own shred of sunset. Leah sat beside me, asked how long I'd be on the island.

"Actually, I'm bound for Rarotonga in the morning."

"Tomorrow?"

"That's right."

"How far is it?"

"About twelve hundred miles," Curt said.

The kid gazed out past the lagoon's edge, and I could feel Curt's eyes on me as he spun the ice in his highball. Leah's men were opposed in every way but misery.

I once did a passage with my cousin Tom and his girlfriend. Maybe our Friday departure jinxed us: ever since Jesus was nailed up, it's been bad luck for sailors. And I'd been warned about odd-numbered crews on crossings, but they seemed tight and Barb was blond and chunky, not even close to my type. The sea plays tricks on you, though. One yachtie friend classifies women by the number of days before you want to drill them. By Day Seven, Barb was looking pretty good, and they'd been fighting. So to piss Tom off she had me show her astral nav, hand on my shoulder as I taught. Only a fool would try something on a small boat, though. Sound carries, and even silence is suspicious. I never touched her, but things got tense between Tom and me the last five days to land. Nothing against women, but they're bad news at sea.

THEY LEFT SAN DIEGO on a Friday. The air was cool but the sun high as they shipped their lines and raced for blue water. The plan was to clear the cargo lanes by nightfall, and with both engine and sail they carved a steady seven knots through light swell. Excitement balled in the kid's stomach, followed by queasiness as the waves deepened offshore. Curt and Leah took separate cabins forward, and after Day One she stayed in hers, even to eat. Curt claimed this was normal, that she would come out when ready. He told the kid about her rich but fucked-up family, how the best thing he could have done was to get her free of them. Curt even joked about how, for lack of privacy, she wouldn't sleep with him at sea.

In the four days it took to reach the trade winds, the kid tried to please him; he wanted to learn, be a salty dog. But Curt hated talking, and teaching even more. Instead, he engaged the autopilot. From that moment on, course changes were made by button, not hand. Thirty-five hundred miles that way; the kid still couldn't believe it. Twelve hours a day baking like raisins because Curt had stowed the bimini to prevent bleaching. He trusted no one and was sick of questions. It was this the kid hated most: Curt's jealous guarding of skills. Then Leah reappeared and things got even worse.

It seemed harmless enough at first. The kid was bored and there was no better diversion than walking the tightrope of double entendre. Night watches became slumber-party chats: he mentioned an ex who hiccuped after orgasm; Leah claimed she'd never had one. But soon their conversation turned from subjects of fun to those of need, and the answers he dispensed so recklessly. . . . He was moved by his own words, and maybe that's why he kept talking. He didn't notice how she memorized what he said for later use because she had all the time in the world.

After a week struggling with dip, azimuth and declination, Curt pronounced the kid a failure and stowed his sextant for the last time. Humbled, the kid returned to his books, surveyed the few notes in his journal. The first subject was the sea of course, just wide enough to swallow all poems written about it. In Week One it lay majestic: wave tops sang promise, hissed adventure beneath their keel. He felt powerful, heroic, and scoffed at those left behind. By Week Two, size had new meaning. He was used to waves but tired of them. The sea was big, ambivalent and very very blue. Their third week under way, his mind bent to just surviving so he could begin anew, re-hatched on Tahiti's far shore.

His plans fascinated Leah. One night, she had him list every dream and then rolled his words in her mouth as though savouring their ambition. She'd never had dreams as a youth, she said, and even now didn't want to try anything new.

"Except stripping, of course."

He stayed quiet, watched the sails draw them farther, a bit farther along.

Five hundred miles north of the equator, Leah began her bathing ritual. Each day she lugged a bucket of water from galley to transom, peeled off her suit and soaped down as he stared off to windward. Curt said nothing about the fresh water she wasted, or the timing of each bath.

Three more days and they crossed zero latitude. Beside celebratory beers, Curt allowed music, and Dylan's *Meet Me in the Morning* sang the kid senseless as he danced on the foredeck. Leah followed him forward; as she started to sway, a gust caught her sarong and bared the dark mound of her pubis. Curt chortled from the cockpit. She kept dancing, hand on her hem. The kid tried to, but his spirit shrivelled, the sight of her sex etched into a brain with too little to do as it was. He despised them, despised himself for the electric thread of excitement she had sown in him anyway.

AT LEAST THE FOOD WAS GOOD. My dorado was fresh and smeared with lolo sauce, the yam served with it soft and fragrant. Colours died on the horizon as Leah kept up her kneading interrogation. I got tired of my own voice, of worrying what Curt must be thinking about his wife's keen interest. As the Aussie cleared our plates, I excused myself.

The washrooms were behind the restaurant, and beyond them was the paved road that circuited Bora Bora's coastline. Before the road, a stone footpath wandered through a garden complete with bench and gurgling fountain. I sat, lit up a joint and let Polynesia work me both inside and out. Tahitian grass is not as strong as the stuff I'd made my living from, but it has a freshness perfect for quiet evenings. As I smoked, the night's fullness grew over me, swept tension aside like a broom.

"Mind if I join you?"

Amidst the flowers and tropical wet, her accent seemed absurd. I made room on the bench and passed the roach, watched her lips purse, inexpertly moist in the soft shine of a lone street light burning from what seemed like islands away.

"Did you enjoy dinner?"

"Very good."

She turned, surprisingly close. "I think you're a nice man, John."

My smile felt lopsided and goofy. I sensed the blood in my face, the twitch of the muscles that ruled it.

"Yes, I like you very much. Do you like me, John?"

"Sure," I said.

Her lips pressed hard, and mine opened, and there was a hand moving on me, slow as stoned logic.

"We could sail together."

How she could whisper while kissing I didn't know, but then her face pulled back.

"Don't you have enough men?" I asked.

"Too old and too young, don't you think?"

Her hand was moving again, and when she curved over my lap it seemed the most natural thing in the world. One should never be without a woman in the tropics. But when my thighs tensed she straightened.

"Shall we go sailing, John?"

I heard my "yes" from a long way away.

She might have kissed me again, but when I returned to the table, she was holding Curt's thick hand and he had ordered another bottle of wine. He seemed energized, his eyes shining as he described Cape Horn and hundred-foot waves, the glory of solo sailing. *Fool shit for fools,* I thought, then spent the next minute wondering if I'd said that out loud. With his beard and curly hair Curt looked classical, an Argonaut in the lamplight. Leah watched me closely, so I leaned back from the table and read some constellations. Leo Major stretched across the night as though leaping, toward or away I could not tell.

At sea only clouds make the night dark. The moon's a spotlight, and with no moon the stars are enough, so thick that you sense the depth between them. One night on my first solo passage there was no wind, and only the mildest swell gave the boat any roll at all. I was in the cockpit with a joint, watching the stars on the water, when it occurred to me that they weren't reflections at all: the boat had flipped and that was sky below me and I was not floating but falling up into space. I was so scared I dragged my shirt through the swells to make certain they were there. After that, I went cold turkey until landfall.

THE NIGHT WAS WARM, but the kid felt cold, and tired of talking. Curt's love for silence was a mystery no longer. Nor did the kid wonder what Leah did in her cabin all day. She was thinking up questions, or the next secret to share.

"Adultery is really not very nice at all, is it? You have to be a really horrible person to do that sort of thing, don't you think?"

Above them, sails glowed like the snow he'd fled long weeks before.

"Maybe I should be a writer. I have lots to write about. One time in Wales I was watching a play, about an Irish poet, I think. I remember thinking that his life wasn't nearly as interesting as mine. I would be a good writer, don't you think? Yes, I should think so: you've been listening to my stories for weeks now."

"Because I'm a captive audience, Leah."

A long pause, then her voice, raw as blistered flesh.

"I think that's *horrible*. You said we were friends. You took my life for *a month*, asking me to come! I didn't want to; I knew it was a mistake and I was right, but you said you needed me and I came. How could you be so mean, saying that?"

He'd heard his words from a distance, as though someone else were speaking them. "If you don't mind, I'd like to end my watch in peace."

For two days Leah was gone again, tucked up in her cabin like contraband. The few times her door opened she fired the kid injured glances, flipped over a new page in her notebook. Once, he heard Curt addressing her in hushed tones, and when the old man stepped on deck he was angry.

"Look, I don't know what's happened with you and Leah, but you must be gentle with her. She likes you, you know, but she's not all right in the head. Just try to be nice; it wouldn't kill you."

"Are we stopping for fuel in the Tuamotus?"

"You know the answer to that."

Curt's boss had forbidden them to stop anywhere but Papeêté. For the kid, the old man's obedience summed up everything that was wrong with navy training.

"We need the fuel."

Curt's face darkened. "Look, you're not going to start becoming a problem, are you? It's my decision, and that's final, clear?"

The kid just stared back, weighing his hatred.

The night they passed through the Tuamotu Archipelago was full of squalls. Dense anvil clouds were backlit by heat lightning swallowed by deep rolls of thunder that began everywhere at once. By morning the wind had died. The kid had never seen the sea so calm, and the nearness of their destination was torture. Four hundred miles to Tahiti and doing two bloody knots.

When Leah reappeared, she was loaded for bear. Subjects discussed weeks ago resurfaced, the kid's words misquoted, misunderstood. At first he tried untangling her, but there was no respite. His answers got shorter, his silences longer as she prattled on. She described how he'd injured her, made life unbearable because she felt so worthless and used. Some nights he would go below, his sole wish that when he returned she'd have vanished, a dark spot on a darker wave. At times he wanted to toss her over himself. Then one night Leah was on the wrong side of the lifelines, leaning over the water as if she had lost something. He watched from the companionway, mind screaming at her to do it, at least this one brave thing in her life. Instead, she turned and looked right at him.

In a flash he was behind her, helping her back into the cockpit, but it was far too late for him. Caught, his guilty arms held her a while, then her face nudged his open like a door.

"Are you my friend?" she whispered.

He nodded, and his lips pressed hard as her tongue slid over his clamped shell of teeth, seeking entrance, that first hairline crack.

TIME TO GO. PUSHING MYSELF up out of the chair, I thanked them for the company and dinner, said how I hoped to see them again, that the yachtie world was a small one, Godspeed, good luck, safe sailing and so on. When I shook Curt's hand, his grip pulsed before releasing me, the curl of a smile on his chapped lips. Leah rose and kissed my mouth, her eyes bright in the lamplight. The kid walked me down to my dinghy.

"Listen, I'm almost out of reading material and was wondering what your library was like. Name like *Soma* you must have something up my alley."

"You're welcome to drop by if you like."

A squeeze on the gas-line bulb, then I yanked the starter cord. The engine caught with a roar and he cast me off.

I'd been aboard *Soma* twenty minutes when the dock lights spoiled the round darkness. The sound of their outboard sputtered across the bay, and from the bow of their dinghy a flashlight swept the water ahead. After the clumsy sounds of unloading, I waited for the engine to start again.

Fact is, most sailors love gossip. Tahiti's too expensive to have a real yachtie community, but backwaters like Tonga and Fiji are the absolute worst. Most folks go to sea to escape, then hit land and find out that gossip's what they missed most of all. A lot of cruisers get somewhere and just park, live cheap like the natives, content in their ex-pat flotilla. I've met people who have stayed ten years in a place. Recent arrivals are like episodes of the same show: tales of breakdowns, breakups, affairs and petty madness. Small things seem to be real important this far from the World. Fifty miles offshore, there seems no World at all.

Yachties are like turtles; your small space becomes your home, your own little universe. At sea, you start thinking only you have the answers, that each thing must be dealt with, that everything, even time, is all up to you. That's a dangerous sort of vanity when you're around people, because you don't hold all the strings. At the end of the day you're only half the conversation.

IT DIDN'T HAPPEN UNTIL LAND. He was still smart enough to wait until there was somewhere to run. They'd spent four days burning the last of their fuel when Tahiti's volcano appeared from sixty miles off. Suddenly all was right with the world. The clouds changed shape on the horizon. Litter dappled the waves. There were birds everywhere, and the kid discovered he could *smell* the land rising to meet them. Dolphins surfed their bow wave, guided them into harbour. Papeêtê wore all the flags of the tourist trade. The shoreline was laced with parked yachts and speeding cars. Diesel fumes rose through the palm fronds, over the cafês and ice-cream parlours and black-pearl vendors. In a few days he'd despise this bustle, but in that moment shore life was the most beautiful thing he'd ever seen.

On terra firma, Curt's personality switched, just like that. He was buying beers, making toasts, everything rosy other than Customs. The yacht's final destination was four islands west, but they could not move until they were cleared. As they waited, Curt showed no interest in exploring the island. He was either on board or at the bar, though he did suggest that the kid show Leah around. Their third night ashore, a local skipper took them all to a real Tahitian club. The place was crammed with locals and an immense Polynesian in tropical print banged out salsa on a synthesizer. Curt lasted five minutes, then flipped out. He told the kid to show Leah a good time, shoved a wad of francs into his hand, and vanished.

The bar was packed with men. Two different ones offered the kid money for Leah as their new friend whispered: "*Protect, protect.*" She loved the attention, and even flirted with her leering suitors. The kid led her to the dance floor, steered her by hands and hips over the cramped space. They were both sweating, the friction of skin strange after so long at sea. By the time they stepped back on the boat, it was past two. Curt snored in his bunk. The kid had not been in bed five minutes when she slid in beside him.

Madness, but she was warm, and though her hands were clumsy they were still hands. Her mouth skimmed his chest, then she moved up, tongue a mollusc, so he slid down on her instead. She smelled like shoreline, but her body seemed disconnected, sensation somewhere else. The kid mapped her with small success, just one more failure as he arched over her, his hand guiding himself because she was tight and nothing mattered but avoiding that tongue, her mouth unfilled as he humped because that's all it was, the end of the longest trip. He pictured Curt and came emptily inside her, all three of them fucked in this last doomed transaction.

BORA BORA'S THREE-THOUSAND-FOOT-HIGH SLAB of basalt rises from the lagoon like a tombstone. That's a fair enough comparison considering these islands are dying a half inch a year. From Tahiti's seven-thousand-foot cone, each step westward is one more stage of sinking until there's nothing but submerged reef, a sudden blip on your depth sounder. There's an island five hundred miles from here that sinks every few years or so, only to reappear with the next burp of its volcano. I was smoking another joint, contemplating how nothing was as solid as it seemed, when I heard the sound of quiet swimming. Two hands reached from shadows and gripped the aft stanchions.

I ducked below and got the kid a towel, let him dry off before passing the joint. He took a haul, and passed it back.

"Interesting mode of transport."

He shrugged. "Had to get out of there quietly."

"Things that bad, are they?"

"You've met them."

"So why not get off? The job's done."

He ran a hand through his bleached hair. "That's what I wanted to talk with you about. You said you were heading out tomorrow."

"That's right."

"How would you feel about crew?"

"You don't have to leave the country to leave a boat."

In the pass, signal buoys blinked Christmas reds and greens.

"She said she'd follow me."

I chuckled. "The graveyards are full of indispensable men."

"What?"

"Never mind. Here."

He sucked on the roach, then flicked it into the sea with a hiss. "You want to hear it?"

"Not as bad as you want to tell it."

He said nothing, young frame poised, waiting. I leaned back against the cabin, lit a cigarette.

"Go on then. Spit it out."

HOURS LATER, MY EYES OPENED and everything followed: I considered nothing but simple tasks, necessary preparations for sea. On deck, I measured each step for maximum efficiency, a machine built for the purpose. After a rigging check by flashlight, I hoisted my dinghy on deck with almost no noise at all. The sun was burning cracks in the mountain when I hit the starter. That or the windlass woke them. As my hook came up, hands reached out and slid back their hatch, her dark head appearing. The kid followed shortly after: he was tying fenders on their beam when I swung my bow around. They were arguing as I neared, but it was not the kid's face or hers that struck me as I slipped past them toward open sea. It was Curt behind them, half out of the hatchway, admiring my escape.

THE CANE FIELD

REHANA DID NOT SEE RAJIV'S LAND UNTIL THE BURIAL. The sun was high and powerful, and Rehana's father, three days dead, lay in a cardboard coffin beside her in the back of a hired pickup. The wind whipped against her shroud, which finally she removed, her long hair trailing behind like a ship's wake. Cane fields stretched between the coast road and sea but still she caught glimpses of water. The truck slowed and turned inland up a hard dirt track. In the distance, the yellow-green mountains of Viti Levu undulated under cloud, then dropped behind the close hills that ringed Rajiv's home like the fingers of a cupped hand.

Rajiv was waiting outside his strange brick-and-wood house and led them to the back of his property. The hole was very deep and very black, the heap of soil beside the grave dark as coffee grounds. There was no breeze, and when the truck came to a stop an overpowering stench rolled over Rehana from the box. She set her jaw, and was stepping down from the truck when her legs buckled.

She did not recall Rajiv carrying her to the house, but when she woke, the sun had nearly set, its weak rays slanting low-angled and orange through the shadeless window. Her body rigid, Rehana took in the crack-walled white room, the tired furniture, the quiet surrounding her. And that *smell*, the dark musk of male from the lumpy pillow, from the thin sheets pulled up to her neck. She reached a hand under her panties, checked between her legs for signs. When the wooden door of the bedroom creaked slowly open she was on her feet, the scissors from the dresser top clenched in hand.

"Mother?" asked a child's voice.

FORBIDDEN TO ATTEND THE BURIAL, Ardi sat among the boxes in the cramped shop apartment. The room felt empty with her mother gone, her grandfather gone forever. With him dead, the place hated them like the rest of Tavua: the women in the street; the girls who pulled her hair, then ran, their faces twisted. With no breeze the air was hot above the store. Outside even the cars sounded angry. Ardi was almost glad to hear the landlord's steps, to hear a voice, but she loathed his gnarled hands, his yellow smile like a dog snarling. When the door chain pulled taut against him, his smile slipped. Ardi watched him through the door crack, his gravel voice rising with anger. Long minutes after he had left, more steps sounded up the staircase, but not the landlord's, or Rajiv's. A man Ardi had never seen called to her, told her to come because Mother was sick. She hesitated, then stuffed a handful of clothes into a bag. *Grandfather*. She could still smell him but the pictures were packed. Nowhere to go but with strangers.

Cruising back along the coast road, the driver asked how Ardi knew Rajiv. All she said was: "He shops at our store."

Ardi could not remember just when she had first seen Rajiv. The man was so quiet and huge it seemed he had always been there, placing money in Grandfather's wrinkled hand, throwing the two fifty-pound bags—one rice, one flour, always—on his wide shoulders as though they were jackets too warm for the weather. Like the rest of him, the giant's face was big. His eyes, however, were small, dark and a bit too far apart. His nose was large, but blunted, as was the round, hairless chin. Aside from his carefully clipped moustache, his whole face had a peculiar quality of softness. To Ardi he just looked peaceful.

By the time the truck reached the cane field, the grave had been refilled. Rajiv stepped from the house, paid the driver, then took the small bag of clothes Ardi carried and led her into the house. He boiled water on the hot plate for tea, and as Rehana slept Ardi told him all she knew. What the landlord had said about the store's back rent, how he had claimed the remaining goods for his own to make up the difference, how they could not afford a real burial for Grandfather. That night Ardi lay curled up beside her still-sleeping mother. The next day Rajiv returned with Ardi's key to the store apartment and loaded their few belongings into another hired truck. He also took two bags of rice and two of flour, leaving money in the otherwise-empty register.

When Rehana finally woke and learned what had happened she was furious.

"Ardi, you never tell a man everything. Never! Do you hear me? Rama knows what he has in mind for us! Did you see all his knives? He'll probably rape me and eat you! You cannot trust them! Any of them. Do you understand?"

That second night, mother and daughter slept again in Rajiv's bed, their boxes piled up against the door. Rehana was awake early the next morning but Rajiv was nowhere to be found, a flat pillow and blanket on the floor the only sign of him.

She woke Ardi, cooked them roti with her father's flour.

"You do not leave this room, understand me? As soon as I go, push the boxes against the door. And don't come out until you hear my voice. There's homework to keep you busy. I'll be back as soon as I can."

Rehana closed the bedroom door behind her, waited for the sound of boxes being stacked, then hurried from the house. She did not like leaving the girl, but the thought of Ardi seeing her beg for help was unbearable. On both sides of the track the cane rose up, a silent, impenetrable wall. The tall stalks swayed the faintest bit in the hot breeze as she strode the long way to the road.

The bus took twenty minutes to arrive, and as she settled into her seat Rehana realized she had never spent a night outside Tavua before. She was anxious to return, but as the bus pulled in, the market and sun-bleached streets looked different to her, harsher. The shadows in corners had a cobwebbed darkness, and the faded store signs and facades seemed to reflect too much light. She normally enjoyed the looks: the narrow-eyed recognition of the town's women, their outrage as she calmly lit another cigarette or stared brazenly back at their men. Even the black-eyed lust from the corner boys had its charm, but not today. Everything was angular, including the landlords. They knew of her, and made no effort to hide their scorn. If they were women they refused her outright; if men, they cast yellowed eyes over her and grinned with rotting teeth. And for the first time, her assurance bruised like skin. Worn and fragile, she retreated to the familiarity of her father's store only to find newsprint-covered windows and a new lock.

The late-afternoon sun brushed the ocean when Rehana stepped back off the bus. The walk over the hill to Rajiv's house was long and shaming. She was not certain whom she hated more: the townsfolk for shunning her, or Rajiv for taking her in. And then there was Ardi. Rehana clenched her newspaper tightly under one arm and toiled uphill. At its crest she froze in her tracks. Below, the field stretched away like a hill-shored sea and Ardi moved across its surface as though swimming, her torso gliding through green. Ardi saw her mother and waved, floated over, impossibly tall and fluid, but when Rajiv stepped from the cane with the girl perched on his shoulders, Rehana's amazement flashed to anger.

"Get down from there! You put her down right now!"

Rajiv's face betrayed nothing as he set Ardi down, watched Rehana grab her daughter's arm and march wordlessly back to the house. Nor did he speak when he returned to find Rehana screwing a thick steel clasp into the door jamb of his bedroom. He sat and ate the roti and rice she prepared, and smiled when she spurred Ardi into the bedroom and locked the door.

REHANA SLIPPED A NEW BUS TRANSFER into the purse on her lap. Only a month old, the purse already had a broken zipper, and the vinyl handle looked ready to part any minute. Her cigarettes were at the bottom, with the advertisement. She cupped both hands around her plastic lighter, let the cigarette's grey heat warm her lungs. The ad was marked with sweat, its coarse paper fluttering between her fingers in the breeze through the bus window.

AUSTRALIAN GOLDMINER
SEEKS INDIAN WIFE
successful 36-year-old w/m seeking wife
(20 or younger) to share new three-bedroom
Melbourne house. Interviews 9 to 3, Buré #5
Vataviti Resort, Tavua

At Tavua's depot, the bus idled in a cloud of diesel fumes and dust. Rehana did not get off. She stayed hunched in her seat, sweating beneath her deep green *salwar kameez*. Across the road, a market's paved square was cross-hatched with painted lines to cordon off one vendor from the next. Slim poles had been erected from which blue and orange tarpaulins hung to shade the Afro-ed Fijian women lolling in once-colourful cotton dresses among taros and dirt-encrusted yams. In sudden darkness beneath a corrugated roof, men shoved past one another like beetles through deadwood as they sold their few wizened peppers and wormholed lettuce heads.

Beyond the market, the tired bustle of Tavua's streets. Indians still ran the town; the bakery and butcher's, the clothing and camera stores. The tinny sound of sitars plinked through blown stereo speakers. Plywood sheeting was nailed over a smashed display window, forgotten shards glinting in the gutter. Wiry, moustached young men, furtive and edgy in dark corners, exhaled smoke that rose past cracked walls and handpainted OUT OF BUSINESS signs.

"Peanuts, *memsahib?*"

Outside the bus window, an Indian girl of thirteen. She wore a dusty school uniform and lifted a brown paper bag hopefully.

"Why aren't you in class?" Rehana demanded.

The girl dropped her gaze and moved farther along the bus. "Peanuts? Peanuts, *sahib?* Only fifty cents."

Rehana scanned the depot. There were children everywhere, twice as many as before, both Fijian and Indian, all selling small bags of nuts, or cigarettes in threes, or one-foot lengths of sugar cane to be tooth-stripped and chewed. *This is what life has come to,* she thought bitterly.

His second cigarette abandoned, the driver slid back behind the wheel, a line of Tavuans in tow. When an Indian woman in a sky-blue sari stepped aboard, Rehana averted her eyes, pretended not to notice. Five stops later Rehana got off, and though the saried woman could not have guessed her errand, Rehana felt dirty, as though smeared with exhaust from the disappearing bus.

Vataviti Resort was almost entirely hidden by palms on the flank of a west-facing hillside. A low-budget hostel, its office was the bottom floor of a two-storey main house, and beside the dorm rooms were several smaller, pandanus-walled *burês* surrounding an empty pool. Rehana checked the *burê* number on the ad again as she moved up the paved driveway. She was just before the door when it swung open and a teenaged girl and her mother stepped out. Wordlessly Rehana took in the girl's gold-embroidered sari, the coiled bangles, earrings and nose ring with its thin chain linked to her earlobe, the blood-red *tilak* between her finely plucked brows. The girl did not look at her, nor did her mother a half step behind. They were past her, gone, and the door frame was filled by the wide bulk of the Australian.

His bathrobe was beige but lustrous, and his gold watch gleamed as he lounged on the loveseat. Rehana sat in the wicker chair across the small coffee table. He had been to Fiji before, the Australian explained, and found the Indian temperament to his liking. The women were well schooled in housekeeping, and they knew how to please a man.

Rehana admired the view out the open porch doors as his gaze moved like fingers over her.

"Did you bring a picture?"

"No, but Ardi is very beautiful," said Rehana.

"Takes after her mother, I reckon. Where's your husband?"

Rehana blushed and looked away. A small fridge hummed in the corner of the room.

The Australian leaned across the coffee table. "Choosing a wife is a bloody tough decision. I'll have to sample the goods, you understand. To know if she's the right one."

He must have noticed her shudder, because the Australian leaned back in the loveseat and smiled. "You know, if she had citizenship, you could apply for landed status within the year."

Rehana said nothing. Even as he led her to the door with instructions on when to return, she could only nod faintly. On her way back down to the road it was as though she were not a part of her body, but floating dizzily just above it.

AMIDST THE STILL CANE, Rajiv was an image in motion. The swing of his upper body, the smooth interchange between cutting and clearing hands was a meditation, without end or beginning. No normal sound could have torn him from his trance.

Rajiv had long come to ignore the barbs of human laughter. But this laughter was more vibration than sound; it trembled down the cane leaves, grew through their twisted roots and sang up his machete as though it were an antenna. He froze, felt the field quiver even as the breeze flowed overland with the first faint rumblings of the trucks. He straightened and watched them creep over the low-slung hills, studied their bulk as they shook and rattled off the broken track across the severed cane stalks toward him. The trucks had come to his field once that day already. As the dozen men jumped from the trailers, Rajiv saw A. J. himself had accompanied them.

A. J. Lowatu climbed down from the cab of the lead truck with the slow assurance of a man who could move fast when he wanted to. As he ambled toward Rajiv, his men fanned across the cut zone and began gathering the severed cane into bunches.

"Christ, Raj. You been dicking around agin. Thought yid be through the lot of it by now." A twitch of a smile as he spoke. No man could match Rajiv's pace. Two couldn't, and both knew it.

"Just gave Ardi a ride in from the road. She's lovely, same as her mum. How old is she, fourdeen, fifdeen?"

Rajiv shifted his stance, but said nothing.

They watched silently as A. J.'s workers slung the tightly wrapped bundles to their shoulders and fed them into the trucks. The men worked quickly. With cane, the longer between cutting and crushing, the less the crop's yield. After a time Rajiv glanced sidelong at A. J., not so much wondering why he had come but when the man would tell him.

There were no wolves in Fiji, but A. J. looked like one all the same. Though he bore his father's dark Melanesian skin, A. J.'s straight silver hair was thick enough that one comb-stroke held all day, and under similarly thick brows his hard eyes were part amusement, part calculation. He spoke English with a perfect Kiwi accent, the legacy of an ex-pat mother and years on New Zealand rugby fields. His fifty-year-old frame had lost little in form or function since his playing days, and at six foot five inches he was one of the few Tavuans not dwarfed by Rajiv. A. J.'s wealth gave him a few extra inches anyway.

All native Fijians inherit land, but since A. J.'s return from New Zealand, his influence had grown a hundredfold. Besides cane farming, he had a hand in housing developments and hostels, and he had led one of the most successful campaigns in Fiji's last election. *"Yes" to Coalition: an all-Indian vote is a wasted vote,* he preached to urban Indians. *The Alliance Party is a defunct colonial legacy. Social programs to benefit the poor. Native chiefs forced to distribute wealth and land more fairly, and more equality for Indo-Fijians. Inquiries into the Alliance's corrupt past. This vote is not about race, but about class and good government.*

He had won his riding by a landslide. But a month ago he had watched Colonel Setvini Rabuka march into Parliament with ten gas-masked soldiers to march out the new Coalition Prime Minister at gunpoint. Now A. J. was back to watching his crew. They were nearly finished gathering Rajiv's crop when he began to speak.

"I have this aunt, Fijian, from my dad's side. She was a nurse, but people go to her for different reasons now. They say she kin see things." He looked sidelong at his tenant. "She was telling me this dream she had, about a cane field with hills around it. One second the cane was standing, the next it was all cut down."

The sun dropped lower, the sky a soft orange beyond the rim of hills.

"Was that all she said?" Rajiv asked quietly.

"She said the cane was bleeding."

The faintest nod from Rajiv's dark head, then the throaty churn of a truck's ignition.

A. J. stood with him a moment longer. "Give my best to your woman." He stumbled over the cane roots toward the trucks.

FROM THE HILLTOP, REHANA WATCHED as A. J.'s trucks rattled down the pocked track to the road. She had avoided the track, using instead the narrow footpath separating the edge of Rajiv's field from the next. Long strides carried her up along the spine of linked hills behind the house, the field, past everything but baked grass, shrubbery and the breeze flowing inland. Once at her lookout she faced westward, head shielded by her *dupatta* against the sun. Not thinking about Ardi, or the Australian, Rajiv, or her father buried below. Not thinking. The trucks' harsh ignitions had snapped her peace, dragged her down to earth as they rumbled off toward the coast road. She heard their gears shift as they pulled out, heading southwest toward the Ba sugar refinery. She could see clouds of vapour lifting from its distant stacks, and the hazed blue sweep of sea beyond them. Everything looked softer from a distance.

She rose, brushed the dead grass from her thighs, and started down the hillside toward the house. Her descent sped the sunset; light dropped behind the hilltop and she was in shadow, the cane towering overhead. A gust of wind followed her down, rattling the hard stalks. Rehana quickened her pace. She longed for the familiar noise of traffic: sharp, comprehensible. The snake-slip of cane leaves sounded too much like whispers: it played tricks on the mind. Melbourne looked like a beautiful city; she had found a tourist brochure to show Ardi that night. When the cane whispered again, she broke into a run.

RAJIV ENTERED AND THERE WAS ARDI, so small with the curly hair. Rehana was not home. It felt soft inside, hot with the fried smell of roti, his father's house built under the hanging-root tree. Still strange things around, their brown chairs, kitchen table and couch that he still bumped into at night. So small her hands. Rajiv was never so small; even when they died he'd been big and maybe that was why. Strong so he could live, keep the field, fight off that cousin who wanted it. Rajiv had been lonely but glad to see him run off bleeding from the flat of his knife; his place, mother and father's place, it was Ardi's place now. Land was yours when you buried yours in it. If she listened closely she'd never be lonely. There was no cruelty in fields. Cane knew no past but soil.

Rajiv leaned his cane knives just inside the door. He had ten of them, sharpened them each night for the next day's chore. Blades dulled quickly on the cane stalks; having several saved him time. He stooped under the door jamb and smiled as Ardi turned to him from the hot plate.

"Mother isn't home, and I need some yams."

Rajiv reached and pulled the chain for the naked light bulb above her, then moved past the bedroom and through the back door.

The garden was nearly as big as the house. One tilled edge was bordered by a round cement cistern, and the broad leaves from the yam stems fanned out across most of the garden's width. Rajiv lifted the shovel leaning beside the door and drove the spade into the ground, pried upward, then drove the blade in again. He stooped and sifted the cool soil until his fingers found the fat, firm bulk of a yam. The roots gave some resistance, but his biceps twitched and he tore them free. He laid the yam gently beside the hole and severed roots and stalk with the shovel blade, then placed them back into the hole and buried them. When he turned to re-enter the house, Rehana blocked the doorway, her slim body tense, backlit by the stark kitchen light.

"I must talk to Ardi about something important tonight. I want you out of the house after supper."

A brief pause, then he nodded. She stepped aside to let him in.

RAJIV WATCHED ARDI'S SMALL FINGERS CURL around her fork as she ate; cinnamon skin, the shell pink of clean nails. Her mother made regular inspections of her teeth, ears, hands, but Ardi's hair caused the most difficulty. Fanned across her narrow back, her thick curls snagged every piece of wind-borne jetsam that passed. They kept it coiled with a ribbon, but at least every other day Ardi was by the cistern lathering, rinsing it clean. Given the drought of recent months, Rajiv worried about the water she was using, but said nothing.

They ate in silence round the small table and, when finished, Rajiv rose and carried his empty plate over to the newly bleached sink. He had given Rehana money to buy what she needed, but bleach was the only thing she had purchased. Bleach and soap for

Ardi's hair. From the small shelf above the sink Rajiv took down the worn grindstone, picked up his cane knives and stepped out the back door.

The night was clear and, without town lights to interfere, the stars cast a faint luminescence over the house and stalks of the field. Rajiv stooped beside the cistern, lifted and filled a small steel bucket a quarter of the way. He straightened and looked around, suddenly uncertain. Usually he sharpened on the back stoop, but she wanted him farther away than that. He stepped carefully around the garden and into the cane, following the path there more by feel than sight. When he found his parents' grave, he set his knives and bucket down and propped himself against the headstone.

They were like breezes; in the field, voices always sounded like breezes at first. He cocked his head, waited for the words to sharpen.

"*. . . body is not holy . . . something to bargain with . . . one thing we have . . . stolen from me. . . . this man likes you . . . anything you want . . . a nice, rich man . . . you will do every . . . don't let him touch your . . .*"

He took a breath and waited, but heard nothing else. Finally he hefted a cane knife, splashed water onto the grind-stone, and drew the blade firmly across the fine grit.

THE SUN HAD NOT YET CLIMBED THE HILLS as Rehana applied the mascara brush to Ardi's lashes. She required very little makeup: a bit of rouge on her fine cheekbones, a touch of fixative to keep her eyebrows combed. The red lipstick was set off nicely by the scarlet *tilak* between her brows. *Just the hair now,* thought Rehana. Washed already, Ardi's curls were far more manageable when wet, and the oil glued them flat to her head under a square of pinned silk. Rehana tucked and folded the red-orange sari around her daughter's shoulders and hips.

"My mother married Grandfather in this sari. It will bring you luck."

Ardi said nothing, just lifted and dropped her arms as directed. A curious numbness stole over her, even as she examined her mother's face.

"Why don't you marry Rajiv?"

Rehana froze, then laughed sharply. "Don't be silly, girl. What has Rajiv to offer? A shack in a field with nothing but rice and yams to eat, that's what! Besides, the land belongs to A. J.! With the Colonel in power, farmers are already being thrown off the land. The blacks take what they want, and soon enough Rajiv will find himself on the street, mark my words." Her hands twisted the silk in upon itself. "And don't let his silence fool you, either. He wants something, sure as the nose on his face! The men here are bad men, and this is a bad place. This Australian is a gentleman, and from Melbourne. Soon you will have your own house, your own car and many wealthy friends."

For a moment, Ardi wanted to tell her. How she was happier here amidst the quiet growth of the cane, but all she said was: "Grandfather is here."

Rehana's face darkened. "Grandfather is *dead*. He *can't help* us any more." Then she smiled. "You are a clever girl, Ardi. You are better than this place. It may seem hard to understand, but not many get this chance. You know how much I have sacrificed for you; you must do this one thing. It is worth it, daughter, believe me." Her voice was gentle as she slipped the gold bangles around Ardi's wrists.

REHANA SAT NEAR THE BUS WINDOW so the wind would not rustle Ardi's hair. She squeezed her daughter's hand reassuringly, but Ardi hardly noticed. She did not feel well. Her stomach had a sickening buzz inside, and the faintest wafts of exhaust from passing trucks made her dizzy. The traffic slowed near Tavua, and passengers up front began craning their necks for a better view. Cars and trucks were parked on both sides of the road. A crowd of mostly Indian men were on one side of a culvert bridge, some with scraps of plywood nailed to makeshift handles, their signs' hastily painted lettering still wet and dripping. *Coalition=Democracy. Rabuka=Nazi.* There was a large pile of scrap metal and wood by the edge of the crowd, and the men were listening to a wiry Indian in a white-collared shirt who was standing on the hood of an old station wagon stripped of all but its tires. Resentment poured through his bullhorn and rose off the crowd with an odour sour enough to make Ardi gag. The bus had just crawled past when the men began pushing the wreck toward the bridge.

Rehana turned to her daughter.

"That is why we must go."

PEOPLE MILLED AROUND TAVUA'S DEPOT. In front of the market the sidewalk was thick with bodies. Rusty cars filled the streets with exhaust, but no one seemed to be going anywhere, or want to. Something was close at hand. Finally their bus pulled free from the congestion and jerked to a halt in front of Vataviti.

Ardi dragged herself up the drive to the *burê*. Her mother's arm stayed fixed around her shoulders, fingers tight on the fleshy part of her arm. *Remember what I told you*, Rehana's eyes warned. Palm trees and frangipani bushes pressed close as she knocked on the *burê* door. Like the jungle, but different.

Ardi knew the unseemliness of looking a suitor in the eye, but as the door swung inward, she could not help a brief glance. The Australian was not a tall man, but he was big. Thick wrists, a rounded middle under the beige terry-cloth bathrobe. His face was wide and sunburned, and beneath a thin blond moustache his wide smile displayed perfect teeth. As Rehana guided her inside, Ardi yearned to ask if he had bought them.

The *burê* porch was bright with sunlight. The pool lay just beneath it, and as she stood at the railing Ardi's numbness was replaced by a sudden urge to swim, to just leap right over the edge.

"They're filling the pool today. It's been empty since I got here."

The Australian's voice did not fit his build. Thin, reedy; only its accent was interesting. Ardi studied his frame: the round, knobbed knees and heavy feet; the coils of grey-blond hair pinched in the V of his robe lapels. He and Rehana both sat down on the plastic deck chairs.

"What's her name?"

"Ardi," said Rehana primly.

"How old is she?"

"Sixteen," her mother lied.

"She's a looker. That's a nice sari, Ardi."

Rehana's eye caught hers, narrowed.

"Thank you, *sahib*," Ardi said.

"Can she cook?"

Rehana leaned forward in her chair. "Oh yes, sir. Very well, and she is a very good student. Ardi learns everything quickly."

The Australian smiled faintly. "Have you been to Australia, Ardi?"

She shook her head.

"It's much bigger than Fiji. You'll like it a lot. I've a big house in Melbourne to live in when I'm not down the bloody mines. There's some pictures inside if you'd like to see 'em." He stood, and held out one thick red hand.

Strange how blue veins look on white people, Ardi thought as his fingers closed around her own.

RAJIV HAD WATCHED THEM from the cane. Rehana walked a step behind the girl to make certain the sari did not drag. A strange tightness grew in his chest as they moved past. He did not stop to wonder what caused this. *She looks like flame,* was his sole thought before retreating to the oiled motion of cutting. Yet the girl's image persisted, the sound of her small voice echoing within the arc of his swinging blade.

The sun had climbed its highest when Rajiv straightened and studied the swath of flattened cane behind him. He was slower today. The weight of this realization settled into his limbs like earth. Rajiv licked some of the clear sugar sap off his knife blade, then jerked the steel back. The liquid was warm but salty, as though sown with sea water. He frowned and slashed the knife down through another stalk. Faint laughter quivered through the ground as he examined the severed shaft, watched as thick white fluid dripped over the roots underfoot.

That is how A. J. found him, motionless, as though rooted to the soil. Only when he slammed the door of the small pickup did Rajiv turn and watch his landlord move hurriedly toward him from the truck.

"Best stop cutting, Raj. The refinery's closed. They're striking. Had the wife on the phone all morning to warn people but forgot you didn't heve one. Came as fast as I could, but some bloody protest blocked off the road through Tavua."

"For how long?"

"The strike? Don't know. Heve to see how the Colonel deals with it." A. J. paused, gave Rajiv a careful look. "The girl here?"

Rajiv shook his head.

A. J. frowned. "I own a hostel on the other side of town. Live in the top floor of the main house. Thought I saw her go into one of the *burês*. That's what reminded me of you, actually. She wearing a sari, an orange one?"

A slight nod from Rajiv's huge head.

A. J. swore under his breath. "Look, when she gits beck you tell her to steer clear of there. That Auzzie's bin here before, and she should keep away from 'im, understand?" He shook his head. "I've got to go, Raj. I'll be beck to let you know what's happening at the mill." He swore again and strode off toward the pickup.

THE AUSTRALIAN ROLLED, checked his watch in the bedside drawer. Three more appointments but not for an hour yet. He watched the girl slip the bloomers back over her slim brown legs. He reckoned she'd been easy enough to unwrap. All except for the kerchief over her hair. He had gone to remove it and damn if she hadn't slapped his hand away. No matter; silk on the pillow had its charm. If anything, that's what he'd remember about this one. He rose and pulled on his bathrobe, checked his watch again. Time enough. Walking over to the girl, he helped her draw the *choli* over her head, kissed her covered hair lightly, then turned and opened the door.

Outside, the mother stood at the porch, hand on throat, waiting. She'd want a smile, then, and he gave her one: faint, noncommittal. He watched her face fall, took a step toward her.

"The girl's a beauty. Very well behaved. You've raised her bloody well." He smiled again, placed a hand on her shoulder. "But I'll be honest; I've met many young girls, all of 'em nice." He paused, his eyes drifting, hand creeping to her neck. "They don't have mums like you, though." He dropped his hand. "Go help her dress. I'll be in in a bit. Maybe *you* can show me why I should take her to Melbourne."

THERE WAS NO TRAFFIC along Tavua's main strip. The soldiers were nowhere in sight, but their spectre remained. Vendors abandoned the depot, and the few people on the street spoke softly, kept to the sidewalk. By decree, only bankrupt shops could close.

Mother and daughter sat in silence as their bus bounced over the culvert bridge. The wrecked car was gone. All that remained of the roadblock was some broken plywood and scraps of corrugated iron on which locals converged, bearing pieces ant-like toward home because there were always holes that needed mending. The few pools of blood were covered with dust.

The bus pulled down the coast road, and Rehana welcomed the breeze through the window. Neither she nor Ardi saw A. J.'s truck roar past in the other lane. They were two stones in a river, numb as the world flowed past. When the bus shuddered to a halt, the driver had to turn and shout to them. They began the long trek up the dirt track. Again Rehana followed a step behind Ardi, and caught her when she stumbled. The girl's face was sickly white. *I wish it were sunset,* was all Rehana could think. The sun was too high, promised too many hours before dark, coolness, sleep. The house's shade was such a relief that she almost wept when they entered.

Rajiv watched them from his chair, his sweat scent blooming around him. When Rehana noticed him at the table she gave a start.

"What are you doing here? Why aren't you in the field?"

Rajiv's gaze settled on Ardi.

"No cutting today. A strike."

"So you just thought you'd sit here and wait and scare us half to death? What kind of a man are you? Why don't you take a walk or something? We need to bathe. Yes, go for a walk. Go on, go!" She took an angry step toward him.

For another moment he studied them. Then he rose slowly from the chair and moved outside.

THE FIRST THING TO GO was the kerchief. Ardi did not want her mother to help, and said so.

Rehana ignored her. "I know that was hard, but it is over now. You are okay." Her deft hands unwound the sari, folding the silk bolt as she went.

Ardi slipped off her petticoat. The wad of toilet paper was still between her legs, stuck fast to the matted curls. *Like my hair,* she thought, pulling the paper away.

Rehana wrapped a threadbare towel around her daughter's middle, tucking the ends over her small breasts.

"You are a good girl, Ardi. Look at you." She turned her to face the small mirror above the dresser. "You are beautiful. You will make a wonderful wife. Now go bathe. You will feel much better, I promise." Rehana kissed her softly on the head.

Ardi moved out of the bedroom and through the back door to the cistern, a cake of soap in her small hand. Compared with the sun's heat, the water was cold as she tipped the bucket over her head. Her vagina stung with the soap, and only after many rinses did the oil wash from her hair, still curly even after this. Behind the house there was nothing but the close hills and cane. Ardi let the towel drop, felt the sun warm her as she stood, shaking.

THE BEDROOM WAS EMPTY when Rehana returned from her bath. She closed the door, unwound the towel and rubbed her black hair dry. If she thought hard enough, she could no longer feel him. Rehana glimpsed herself in the small mirror, and moved closer to examine her face. Her lip was swollen where she'd bit down, but the bleeding had stopped. Taking a step backward, she admired the curve of her throat. *You cannot break me,* she thought. Rehana was halfway across the room before the cut was too small for her to see.

Scissors.

The dresser top was bare and Rehana flew from the room. Ardi lay curled into a ball at the foot of the bleached sink. *Blood?* No, dark strands over the floor, but when Rahana screamed Ardi leaped away and out the back. Rehana fell to her knees, gathered the hair to her. When the light from the doorway was blocked by

Rajiv's huge frame she climbed naked to her feet, strands stuck to her legs, her breasts, screaming: *"Is this what you want? Is this it?"*

FOOTPRINTS IN THE GARDEN. Rajiv followed Ardi's path into the cane. His pace quickened when her trail met his other, older one, then halted before the small clearing. Her head rested on their gravestone, a towel drawn over her like a blanket. He stepped toward her slowly, for the first time hating his size, how he frightened them. She did not move, even as he lifted and held her, so light in his arms.

"Tell me."

THE AUSTRALIAN CLOSED the *buré* door behind the last mother and daughter, then checked his watch. Eight forty-five. He did not usually make appointments so late, but they had come all the way from Nadi. Besides, this was his last day here, thanks to A. J. Stupid cunt had barged in like a water buffalo, wanted him gone in the morning. A bit late for a crisis of conscience, he'd told him.

He opened the sweating bar fridge, took out a bottle and moved through his porch doors to the railing. A palm-mounted spotlight shone into the dark-blue hole of the pool. A. J. had begun filling it that afternoon, and the deep end already had four feet of water, ripples bright as cane blades in the light. Across the road, the ocean was only a hundred yards distant. The Australian breathed in salt air and caught the scent of something else, sharp, like dirt-laced sweat.

RAJIV HAD BEEN WALKING a long time, but how long he did not know. Hard steel in hand, he knew only that at first it was daylight and then the sun slipped and fell and overhead, darkness spread like an oil spill. Beneath stars, the night was burning. Farmers had lit the cane roots; flame encircled Tavua like the fires of an enemy camp. But people were drawn by the sirens. Outside the tavern, the victim was cut but breathing, the stabber raging as he was shoved into the rusting squad car. Skirting the echoing street, Rajiv witnessed none of this. No one saw him pass.

Along the road there was no wind or whispers but Rajiv heard cane dying, lying wasted. As he slipped among the *burês*, the salt air was smoky from fires; they were torching roots to turn under, burning to grow. Ash fell in flakes into the pool, and an Indian woman watched from a *burê* porch, her arms crossed like a harness. When the door swung open behind her, she turned, then held the girl who emerged. Rajiv waited for them to go, for the Australian to appear. Too late for them, too late for him. Some men were good for soil, nothing else.

THE FIRST MOTION OF LOVE

Mr. C. K. Stead
1011 Byrant Street
Christchurch, New Zealand

Dear Mr. Stead,

A symptom of too many books as a child is the belief you can live in one, where each journey has a beginning, an end, and resolutions as inevitable as the next chapter. I'd been in Fiji four weeks when I woke beside a rose-scented woman on someone else's yacht and realized my travels had evolved past some superfluous and sequential string of adventures into life. I left Canada fifteen months ago and there *are* stories plotting a path over long blue miles of ocean, but what this letter concerns is stories read rather than written, and those still to be written.

Mr. Stead, I had never heard of you before, but your collection *The Blind Blonde with Candles in Her Hair* impaled me with truth. In a few stories you articulated the most important elements of my life; in fact, you may have even saved my life. But I do not want to get ahead of myself, nor discuss my proposal until we have been properly introduced.

First, my presence in New Zealand. Fate brought Mary and me together in a heat-sink jazz club in Suva, Fiji's capital. She and her two Kiwi girlfriends were vacationing, and I escorted them back to the yacht I had recently been hired to tend. Despite her youthful appearance, Mary is much older than I; her every move bespeaks experience encapsulating a loving and generous core. Judging by the sheer number and variety of male guests brought aboard over the following week, her girlfriends shared this philosophy, but I was too smitten to worry. Indeed, their stay represents the most pleasurable and educational week of my life. The day I returned to find Mary, her friends, as well as the yacht's more fenceworthy items gone was a hard one. However, her note's claim that, had she stayed any longer, love would have made leaving impossible, affected me deeply. For the remaining week aboard I drained the few bottles left in the shattered bar, and wept with longing. Oh, her taut thighs and acerbic tongue! Both my heart and the yacht's carpeting bore scars from our torrid affair, and I nearly wept with joy when, on their return, my employers had me extradited to the country of my choice on grounds of solicitation and gross negligence. Rather than return east, I followed love west.

Your book jacket did not mention just where in New Zealand you are living now, but for an Albertan from the wide expanse of the prairies, N.Z. is a small place. Tell me, Mr. Stead, can a town with a few pleasant acres be considered picturesque? Yes, Keri Keri has that pretty little valley with the river, marina and New Zealand's oldest stone building, but what else? One-level shopping plazas. An abridged main street. It was a point of pride for me that in the week spent with Mary, I never once set foot in the Old Stone Store. After all, I'm a traveller, not a tourist.

I should add that Mary was overwhelmed to see me. After gunning back a second Scotch, she had me explain just how I'd used the yacht's cellphone bill to track her down.

From Auckland, I'd taken the bus north, then hitched a ride from the Keri Keri station in an old troop carrier full of beefalo. On seeing the address I'd written down, the driver grinned toothily, and remained silent for the rest of the ride.

The afternoon sky was mottled with cloud as I laid my pack over the barbed-wire-topped security fence of Mersdan Estate. Inside, the rolling grounds were lined with rows of fruit trees, and moving between them were a half dozen of the most beautiful women I've yet to see in New Zealand. With wicker baskets slightly larger than their bonnets, they wore sleeveless cotton dresses, their long arms sun-browned and graceful as they stretched for the ripe fruit dangling above. When I asked where I might find Ms. Frussett they pointed toward the villa just visible through the trees. Their giggling chased me downhill. A flock of ducks winged the air overhead, splash-landing in the pond behind the long, low building. Only as I beat the knocker on the huge wooden door did I realize that a similarly huge, moustached Maori stood just a few steps behind. He was dressed entirely in black and was utterly silent. After recovering from my surprise, I explained my errand. He disappeared into the villa for some minutes, then returned and bade me enter.

The villa was wide and airy and built from eucalyptus, lava rock and mortar. The foyer looked more like a hotel reception than a home; a striking blonde at the front desk stored my bag in the capacious coatroom. Farther inside, a bar bordered a fireplace seating area, behind which stretched a long, kauri-wood dining table. The whole back wall of the villa was full-length windows overlooking an expansive patio where several couples sat lunching. The men were well groomed and older, the women various but stunning. On the grass beyond the patio, two more women lay nude, tanning on lounge chairs. From one swinging door, a waitress in halter top and stretch skirt emerged with a tray of canapés. Her stiletto heels snapped like gunshots on the stone floor as the Maori led me through another heavy door.

Marianne Frussett was an attractive brunette in her late forties with a languid, regal air. It was amazing: just her taking my hand made me feel my troubles were over. After fixing us drinks from her private bar, she bade me join her on the plush couch near the picture window. Past the pond, vine-lined hills leaned into the horizon. A long, angled mirror beside the window reflected the patio scene back to us, but I was too awed by Marianne to question its purpose. Everything about her spoke of class and fine breeding. With a few minor edits, I explained my situation, which she nodded at sympathetically. It seemed Mary did occasional massage for her at the spa, and she well understood the girl's rebellious and independent ways.

Over our patio lunch of calamari and crisp sauvignon blanc, Marianne described her operation. The combined vineyard, orchard and spa was a favourite of rich and famous men from New Zealand and beyond. There was no place like it for esthetic beauty and quality of service, something I might remind Mary of when I saw her. Then Marianne said farewell and good luck, and minutes later I was sitting beside her still-silent assistant in a black Mercedes sedan speeding toward Keri Keri.

I shall never forget Mary's face when she opened the door. Her eyes widened into dinner plates, mouth so agape that the hand-rolled cigarette stuck to her lip flipped down and seared her shining chin. She spit it out, cursing, but being barefoot could only stare as the butt burned into the welcome mat between my dusty boots. As I ground the ash under my foot, Mary glanced over my shoulder and saw the Maori poised beside the big sedan. She yanked me inside, slammed the door, then raced dizzily around, sliding bolts and drawing blinds. When she finally turned to me, her first words were not of love or even "hello," but a warning never to go near Marianne or the Maori again.

Mary's house is a small, rotting bungalow in an equally decrepit ghetto immured by natives. Perhaps disappointment was inevitable after the splendour of Mersdan Estate, but truthfully, I had expected more from the woman I loved. The carpets were drab, the walls clean but marred by the abrasions of time. With its candle-lit corners, red walls and blackout curtains, the therapy room was by far the nicest in the house, if a little overdone. The table at its centre looked far wider and plusher than the models I'd lain on at other spas, but was no doubt functional.

Mary was concerned what neighbours thought of her, so would not let me play the stereo too loud. She was also obsessed with cleanliness. I washed my whiskers carefully down the cracked enamel sink. I swept up my errant crumbs. I fixed a piece of tape to the underside of the toilet seat with the word *down* written on it as a reminder. Once, I made the mistake of walking nude to the kitchen for a glass of milk. Mr. Stead, I have never lived with a lover before, but walking naked always struck me as an important freedom, a defining part of independence. She made no complaints when her clients did so.

The men who visited Mary were an intriguing mix of what New Zealand has to offer. From big-boned, black-haired Maoris to transparent-skinned colonials, all her clients seemed uncomfortable, almost furtive while answering my queries. As they padded sock-footed down the hall, I was repeatedly stunned by the way men concerned with muscular tension could remain so ignorant of hygiene. I did not learn much from these characters, and considered it no great loss when Mary forbade me to speak with them, or, finally, to be anywhere near the house while she worked.

Exploring Keri Keri took half an afternoon, and having spent the last of my savings on bus fare, I did not have the funds to venture farther. Mary gave me the keys to her Honda, but my favourite place was on the porch outside in sunlight or dark, reading, listening, breathing silence.

> *I've always been drawn to strong, intelligent, verbal, not to say literary women, as some men are drawn to rock-climbing, or hang-gliding, or canoeing down rapids.*
>
> —C. K. Stead, *The Blind Blonde with Candles in Her Hair*

As was I. Mary was a departure, a gorgeous soft anomaly in my regulated web of a life. There are times, as I'm sure you know, when one feels ready for something, waits poised on the brink of some great revelation about life, though we may not know exactly what that thing might be. There are also times when this revelation becomes embodied in the figure of another human being, a standing, breathing, sensual piece of creation. Amid the sun and sand of our tropical paradise, I so admired her self-possessiveness and sense of freedom that I fell in love as much with Mary's approach as with the woman herself. I sought to embrace a new way, to open myself to love.

But there can be cruelty to closeness. What could be worse than having the thing you travelled thousands of miles for finally denied you when it is mere inches away? C. K., I will not ask you whether you have walked in my shoes; for the worldly, such experience is no doubt inevitable. There is no deeper solitude than being both intimate and completely misunderstood, is there, my friend? I was halfway through the ancient kauri forest of Waipu when a wave of sadness overwhelmed me. Afloat in Fiji, love had been our language. A simple touch was enough to imply meaning in all its subtle fullness. On land, Mary seemed a different person, as though sharing hearts was different from sharing a home; as though, after everything, I had no real right to be there. Weaker men would have given in entirely to despair. Instead, I raced back to the car and sped home. So determined was I to fix what was wrong, to preserve the love dissolving inside me that I tripped over the large pair of boots in the front foyer.

What I found will haunt me to the end of my days. Dressed in a loosely tied bathrobe, Mary sat bonelessly before the television, rolled cigarette in one hand, glass of red wine in the other. The room was laced with pot smoke; another cigarette burned in the ashtray by her elbow. I was halfway to the couch when the reverberating chord of a fart seared the air. But I recall these details only in retrospect. My eyes were riveted by her wine, by the three fat ice cubes floating on its purple surface. As I stood, frozen, the toilet's whoosh behind the bathroom door perfectly summarized my emotions. I turned and fled, not bothering to slam the door.

Now, I know what you're thinking. But as a writer, you are acquainted with symbolism, and how in a writer's mind, one thing—even a small thing—can mean *everything*. Since the day I arrived, a list of Mary's foibles had been forming in my mind. Dope before sex. Music during sleep. Salmon on toast. Herpes. In the steamy embrace of new love, such idiosyncrasies are unimportant, charming even. But in the cooler climate of my arrival, I found myself making more and more allowances. In short, indulging her. To err is human, to forgive, divine, but, my God, *ice in red wine?* The irony was that, with no place to go or friends of my own, I was forced to appropriate hers. As I sped toward Mersdan Estate, the landscape that swept past the windows was foreign, surreal. I felt both exhilarated and destroyed, stoned with emotion. Perhaps this explains why, as I drew up to the locked gate, my foot hit the accelerator, not the brake, and the car plowed right through.

By the time the Honda stopped outside the villa, I too was a wreck. The Maori showed me inside, ham-sized hand on the scruff of my shirt. When Marianne spread her arms to greet me, I burst into tears. Even after the fifth gin and tonic, I did not explain just what had happened: I *could* not. I feared she might not understand symbolic import, and find me ridiculous and fickle. All I said was that I had seen something, that it was over, finished. To my relief, Marianne took pity, and took me in. The Maori returned

Mary's blunted but driveable car, and fetched my rucksack of belongings. The spa employees listened attentively to my woeful tale. Amber, the resident redhead, seemed particularly concerned and sympathetic, even giving me a free massage.

But that night, as I lay alone in a four-poster bed looking through my window, the true gravity of my plight took hold. The moon threw a cold, silver sheen over the pond and grapevines, the dark fringing hills. Everything was foreign, even the sheets, and I began to shake like an infant, asphyxiated by the unfamiliar. Slipping from my room, I snuck along the hallway to Marianne's small library. Here I found comfort in the old places. John Donne, Oscar Wilde; I read Eliot's "The Love Song of J. Alfred Prufrock" aloud and wept through the fifth stanza. It was on that same shelf where I found you, C. K., standing with the others in their sombre rows, title tattooed down your spine, your hand-scrawled dedication to "M" for her "warmth and hospitality." And from the first story, the first *sentence*, I heard your thoughts as if they were my own: honest, direct, delving for truth.

> *One wants to say that things are like other things—a sky like lead, or pewter, and the snow falling out of it like confetti, or the petals of white roses. But if you grew up, as I did, in a place where snow never falls, then perhaps you recognize more clearly its uniqueness. That kind of sky is like nothing but itself; and snow falls only like the falling of snow.*
>
> —C. K. Stead, *The Blind Blonde with Candles in Her Hair*

You cannot know what a thing it was, to read this on that cruel April night. After fifteen months away, I saw again the shadows of the riverbank climb the opposite shore, the factory chimneys downriver cast white smoke into the icy blue over frozen water. And far in the distance, a single gas flare. I knew it was Edmonton before you told me. In a dark library in a near stranger's house ten thousand miles from my home you gave me back to myself, and this I will never forget.

Not until the next morning was I caught wriggling on the pin of your implicit questions. I read and reread your descriptions of Alberta, yet it was those observations about writing in Canada that continued to question and fascinate. Strange how in all the CanLit courses I have surveyed you come the closest to nailing down the negative reinforcement of the Canuck identity. Perhaps that is the answer, the ironic realization that our "anti-identity" is so elusive that it can be articulated only by those outside it. How perfect. No, how perfectly *Canadian*.

That same day I wrote my first short story: the tale of a young sailor who follows his heart to New Zealand only to find that his lover works in a brothel masquerading as a spa. In tribute to your inspiration, I even made you a character at the whorehouse! For a solid day I honed, pared, polished. Then I offered the manuscript up to the one person I could trust.

The next morning, Marianne was too busy to visit with me, in fact something serious must have been on her mind because she seemed withdrawn. Her one question regarded my intentions with the story. Naturally I said I wanted it published. She remained scarce the rest of that afternoon and night, but the Maori seemed suddenly ever present.

My last day at Mersdan began beautifully. Over a light breakfast with Amber, Marianne appeared and suggested an ocean-fishing trip with her assistant. I was about to agree when

Amber explained my help was needed in the orchard, and implored Marianne to postpone the trip until that afternoon. Marianne yielded, and soon I was being escorted through the trees by the same six nymphs I'd stumbled across on my arrival. The morning was clear and warm with the climbing sun, but the women were unusually quiet as we strode through the orchard toward the broken and now chained security fence. I was about to ask what was wrong when Amber drew a cellphone from her basket, spoke a few curt words into it, then re-hid the device. Seconds later, the bent grey nose of Mary's Honda crashed again into the gate, the chain snapping like string. Opening the passenger door, the women shoved me inside, and tires squealing, Mary and I rocketed back through the twisted gate.

Certain people should not bother lying. They do not grasp how the most effective lie consists mainly of truth, and subtlety wins the day. As we sped down back road after back road, Mary's tale about Marianne's plan for me was so ridiculous that her true motivation became obvious. That she would go to such lengths to win me back was touching, but as we screeched to a halt in front of the Keri Keri bus terminal, I attained total clarity. In that Zusammenhang, I saw I sought women like countries, desperate to belong. But to become a part of anything—place or person—you must first learn your own soul's landscape. Like writers do. Like you do.

I reflect on the person I was a year ago and scarcely recognize him. How blind he was, how full of conceit. C. K., your stories have shown me sensitivity and subtle skill. I want to meet you, to learn from you. Your words have brought me this far; please, take me the rest of the way. I ask not only for myself, but also for a nation whose tragic lack you yourself have recognized.

You may quite rightly ask what I offer in return. As a father, you have raised and written the stories of your three children as well as any parent can. Well, C. K., I offer another sort of story: unsolicited, bedraggled, yet full of promise. My commitment to be a writer is total. I will follow your instructions to the letter. You have been writing stories a long time, my friend. When was the last time you helped write a *life?*

My second offer relates to those words you have already written about my country. Your description treads softly and beautifully, but there are things you don't know about snow. You don't know what it was like as a child to walk out after a sound, fretless sleep to find your world draped with a blanket to build with. You may not have noticed how with the first snow of the year a wind's soft breath is invisible but for the angle of the flakes. And how the trees, the Alberta poplars violent with gold, keep their fire, shake off the white like dogs drying themselves, their life's heat melting flakes as fast as they land. It took me twenty-four years to learn a tree's latent heat. And what about newness, how snow collects on the most dismal of scenes to erase its sins like a blessing, in one great Hail Mary of white?

In exchange for not setting foot in Keri Keri again, Mary gave me money to go. This last stroke of reverse psychology was as transparent as it was generous; nevertheless I took advantage. Already my course to you was plotted. Once the bus reached Auckland, I phoned Marianne for your address. Currently, I am at Lake Taupo, and will be in Christchurch early next week. Marianne has sent her Maori assistant down with my belongings.

I look forward to meeting you, your sons, and Debra, your loving wife. At the least I might provide an intriguing hour in an otherwise average Kiwi day. At the most you may discover how well some strangers know each other.

Yours faithfully,
Bryce Mallard

THE LEGEND OF KUOP

Once Uman was Kuop, but long before then it was a nameless mountain rising from reef-ringed sea. The reefs had been mountains themselves once; they had boiled from the waves before ocean began drowning them a fraction at a time. But back then, this one mountain had been higher than the rest, and when the rock split and the top cracked open like some monstrous clam, the peak grew higher still.

The two spirits that emerged had no names or form; they changed, shifted like clouds in the wind. They grew fins to cut through water, sometimes wings for the air. As they moved from island to island, reef to reef, these spirits changed many times. After each transformation, their past shape took form behind them until the sky was full, the sea boiling with life. Yet the spirits both knew their work was unfinished.

The land was different now. Though the stone wore soil and trees, the palms leaned over the waves as though looking for answers, for something they lacked. Sharks ruled the water, the frigate bird the air; nothing stalked shores and forests but crabs and lizards tired of water. So the spirits swam south to the cradle of an atoll in the lee of the main lagoon. When they crawled up the beach they found their fins were no use in the sand, their wings too long for the jungle growth. Deep in thought, they drifted in different directions, changing, shifting. Their fins wore down and widened, then split at the ends into digits. Fish scales, so heavy and hot, peeled off against the rocks. Their feathers grew worn and dirty, and broke on the jungle branches. When these spirits rejoined, the sun was low, the dusk heavy with smells from falling tide. They had no wings or armour, just smooth naked darkness balanced on limbs taut with muscle. Both had hair as black as frigates but one's was longer: it rained over two swells of flesh the other lacked, down to the dark centre of her own lacking. They moved closer, exploring with eyes and hands they barely understood, and finally sank to the still-warm sand to learn the cure of their imbalance.

Beginning's End

There were ten children in all: five girls and five boys. They grew quickly on coconut and crab downed with palm water and breast milk. So absorbed were their parents with tending them that the world around grew wild. The frigates learned to steal. Fish, nesting sticks—the birds stole all they could, but never dared touch the infant souls crawling over the beaches, nor did the sharks snatch the little ones from the waves. These creatures feared their creators the same way the spirits feared the now-frequent rumbles from the mountain lurking to the north. The mighty hinge of its cap flexed with dry peals of thunder until, one night, it slowly began to close. As the spirits gathered their children in their arms, a strange wind began to suck from the mountain's mouth. They clung with terrified hands as all were drawn up and over water, then the spirits tore free and threw their kin far away from the gaping maw, themselves consumed with a crack that shook the whole small world.

Seeds

The children scattered over the lagoon. The girls fell on distant islands like Tol, Polle, and Udot. The boys fell faster, to the islands of Moen and Fefan, Tonoas and Tsis. Each one had an island, but as they grew older their solitude grew heavy. They remembered brothers and sisters, and began to search for them on rafts and crude dugout canoes. As their islands were closest together, the boys found each other first. They fished and feasted and devised tests of skill and combat, but all felt a fire inside, pushing them back to the sea for their sisters. From Moen, they paddled together and reached Udot in a day, pitching camp beneath the palms as the sun slipped into the sea.

The First Flower

The brothers were tired from their journey, but Salat was stronger than the rest and not content with sleeping. He walked without purpose, tasting the night as the moon leaped from cloud to cloud like a dolphin. When a trace of woodsmoke touched his nostrils he knew it was not his fire; that was far downwind. Salat searched the beach for miles, finally spotting a faint glow on the ceiling of the forest canopy a few short steps into the jungle. He crept silently, taking care not to rustle the ferns or break through the rotten palm trunks underfoot. He had almost reached the fire when he saw her, curled beneath a blanket of palm fronds. To Salat nothing could have been more beautiful, and as he lay down beside her he did not know whether to wake her and bare his lonely soul or simply watch her sleep so peacefully.

Sunlight woke him, but Salat did not open his eyes. The skin of his face tingled, the sensation growing down his neck and chest. When he finally looked, her hand stayed upon him, nor did her eyes waver when he reached for her. Their union was gentle, clumsy, inevitable. Salat's cry startled birds into flight, and in his strong arms Param bit his shoulder against the pain that tore through her loneliness forever.

The Rape of Param

The pair were still basking in their discovery when they heard voices from the beach. He rose and led her through palms into sunlight. Salat's brothers ignored his greeting; they were too entranced by the unknown beauty holding his hand. All agreed a feast should be prepared to celebrate this reunion. At their camp Param admired the cunning of their canoes, their strength to brave the waters. Each brother believed she was speaking to him alone. They quickly split off into different directions to fish, all determined to return with the largest and most heroic catch.

Param slipped back into the jungle to gather coconut and fruit. As she worked, she found herself humming, and when she placed a hand over her belly there was a new warmth spreading there, like sun-warmed sand. Already she longed to be back with Salat, and she smiled to herself when footsteps approached stealthily behind her. Turning, Param found not her lover, but Ungo, from the island of Fefan. He was smaller than Salat, his limbs wiry. In a wink he had dropped his fishing spear and stood before her, close enough that she could feel the hunger in his bones, the danger. When she stepped back Ungo caught her wrist, his other hand clutching crablike at her body. He threw her to the ground, ripped away her skirt of leaves and wedged himself between her thighs.

The canopy smothered her screams. It was so different; what had been the end to her longing was now cruel and twisting, a new world of pain. Then he was gone. Param was afraid to open her eyes until she heard the sound of blows. She raised her head to see Ungo lifted and thrown across the clearing. Salat closed distance with a hunter's calculation, but Ungo climbed to his feet clutching his fishing spear. He feinted twice, and when Salat thrust forward again his arm brushed the point past and twisted the spear away. The brothers stood frozen, the spear tip hovering near Ungo's skinny throat. Then Salat snapped the shaft over his knee and Ungo vanished into the trees.

Shark Calling

Salat stayed with Param until she slept. He covered her in fern leaves, then began to move soundlessly through the jungle. When the smoking remnants of the campfire came into view, he listened for signs of his brothers, but there was nothing, just the measured rush of sea-swell rinsing the white sand. Two canoes lay beached near the treeline: a heavy three-man dugout and a smaller one. The first had been fashioned by them collectively to cross the big water. The smaller canoe was built by Salat's own hand, large enough for two and the most seaworthy of all solo efforts. Salat knew that he could not simply take the canoe. His brothers fished on both sides of the camp: they would see him and give chase, and three men paddling were faster than one, no matter how strong. So he waded into the water and began to slap the surface with his hands, chanting a mantra to the waves. Soon, quick shadows could be seen in the shallows near him: three, four, six, a dozen. Fins knifed the waves. There were black-tip, white-tip, and grey reef sharks. Up to his waist in water, Salat could feel their rough skin curve between his legs, but these hunters would not attack one without fear, and he whispered his request.

Salat's Escape

Ungo saw him first, paddling across the flame trail of the setting sun. He had positioned himself amidst his brothers, and when he raised the alarm they raced back to camp, grabbed their paddles and heaved the big canoe into the waves. After only a few strokes Ungo noticed the fins. The water seethed with shadow, and the deeper they got the more numerous the sharks became. His brothers stopped paddling, wondering aloud what could cause such a schooling. It was all Ungo could do to get them to renew the chase, but when their paddles bit water the canoe felt sluggish, content to sit where it was. Even their paddles grew heavy and cumbersome. Stabbing into the next wave, Ungo caught a flash of silver. Attached to his paddle were two remoras, the silver-black pilot fish forever clinging to sharks. With a shout he pulled the blade toward him, tore them free and renewed his paddling. By the next stroke there were three more, stuck fast and shining in the sun's orange light. Ungo threw down his paddle and leaned overboard; the entire hull from the waterline down seethed with remoras, all swimming backward, pushing the canoe toward the beach. As he watched, a large black-tip shark cruised past and the remora riding its belly broke free and joined the mass. Raging, Ungo raked his blade across the hull, decapitating two remoras, dislodging several more. He never saw the shark that struck back, but the shock nearly broke his arm along with the paddle, now ripped to kindling in his hands.

No words were spoken as the canoe was pushed calmly back to shore. When the hull struck sand Ungo raced along the beach, screaming for the others to follow. But they were too late. All they found were the marks where Salat had dragged his dugout ashore before relaunching it. There was no need to look for Param. The brothers stood on the beach as Ungo's bitter curses chased Salat's disappearing canoe.

Broken Chain

The next morning the brothers woke with a renewed sense of urgency. Param had given their desire solid form; they coveted what they hardly understood. Wordlessly, each brother began building his own canoe. Ungo finished first and struck out for Ulalu to the northwest. Two others made for the larger islands of Tol and Polle, separated by the narrowest of channels. The last brother searched for weeks before finding his wife on the small, flat island of Tarik. All that remained on Udot was the large, abandoned canoe. The elements took mercy on the craft. Rather than crack it with heat, they sent waves to wash silt over the now-rooted hull, and in time it became an outcropping of stone, the sole reminder of solidarity between Kuop's lonely sons.

Naming an Island

A mile to the north of Tarik was another island, larger but similar in contour. This was where Salat paddled on the night of the escape. When Param woke on a bed of ferns she recalled little of the passage: just a brief surfacing to an explosion of stars, the rocking of waves and the sound of Salat's paddle like a soft, steady pulse. This would be her last journey. Amidst the huts and palms, fruit and fish, she bore twelve children before dying in the still-strong arms of her aged husband. He buried her between the roots of a massive eucalyptus tree. Salat passed on shortly after, but not before giving the island her name.

Convergence

The human weed grows faster than most. The first families spread over their islands until some had no room left at all. Those of Tol and Polle crossed the narrow channel on bridges of trade and marriage. But on the smaller islands the strongest and cleverest descendants began to look eastward toward their father's islands. One day, Tonoken, eldest grandson of the Tarik clan, crossed the small water to Param in search of a wife. The two islands had developed a close association much like that between Tol and Polle. Tonoken had last visited the island two weeks previous, and he was surprised to find four new and finely hewn canoes waiting on the sand where he beached his dugout. No one came to greet him, and he moved stealthily toward the village, half afraid of ambush in the eerie stillness.

He had reached the first row of huts when he heard voices. The entire Param clan was gathered in the clearing at the centre of the village, the women sitting or nursing infants while the men stood and shifted and spoke in challenging tones to one another. One man stood out above the rest. He was tall and wider at the shoulders than his fellows, and his words cut cleanly through the cloud of muddled voices.

". . . do not content yourself. You know our stories; this island has been a safe refuge, but it is not our chosen place, not our birthplace. We outgrow it already. We must reclaim our land eastward. It is time to build, to strengthen. Others do this already."

An old man called out in a cracked but challenging voice: "Why have us move when we are content to stay? We have all we need. Our grandmother lies buried here and protects us."

"Just as our grandfather lies at sea and protects us." The young man's voice dropped so those around him were forced to lean closer. "Why leave here? I will tell you why, Uncle. I have paddled for weeks. I have seen other islands and people. I have drunk and danced with them. And I have fought them." He fingered a recent scar etched into the brown skin over his ribs. "Ungo's grandson gave me this before I killed him. We are at heart a peaceful people, but Ungo's spawn have sworn vengeance upon the sons of Salat. When they grow strong enough they will find us."

"So you would hide, then? Is that your plan?"

"No, Uncle, I would build. Find better soil, and land where we can spread and grow and defend if we must." He drew himself up to his full height: "I want to return to the mountain and claim it."

A murmur rolled through the clan.

"Tumuital, the mountain is cursed!"

The young man smiled grimly. "You say cursed, but we know the same story. The mountain has power, but I say its power will give us strength. We shall kneel at its feet so our children grow with its magic around them, and the clans shall *know* our power."

His words wheeled in the air like frigates and Tumuital leaned eagerly toward his family. "Who will go with me? Come, brothers, step forward and claim your proper place as men."

But there was only silence, and from his half-hidden position Tonoken felt them withdraw like ferns from a fire. He looked again to this strong man alone and his soul leaped into his throat, forcing his words out clear and strong.

"I will join you, though you do not call me brother."

All eyes turned to him as he stepped out into the open.

"I value spirit as well as blood, son of Tarik." Tumuital threw a withering look over those gathered. "Perhaps more so. You are brother indeed."

Tumuital clasped his hand firmly before turning back to the others, already rising to their feet.

Reunion

Six days later the voyagers departed. Two more canoes had been made; a total of sixteen men and ten women set off over the waves. The first day was hard. When they reached Moen, Tumuital let his people rest as he and Tonoken surveyed the island. The highest peak was a thousand feet above the water, and as they stared across the lagoon Tumuital turned to his ally.

"You were not from my island, but that day your courage was the highest mountain on it."

"Highest next to yours," Tonoken said with a smile.

Tumuital shook his head.

"It is one thing to challenge others with a dream you believe in. But to believe in another man's dream, to see and seize the future in a moment . . ." He gripped his friend's arm firmly. "This is not our island, but I will see this peak bears your name."

Some hours after sunrise, their party entered the narrow pass between Tonoas and Fefan. Reefs were everywhere but easily seen. The wind and swell picked up when they slipped out of the lee of Eten, but the hulk of Kuop drew them on. They came in silence, and silence greeted them as they stepped into the trees to strike camp. They ate fresh fish they had caught along with the taro they had stored for the journey. That night, they slept like timid lovers afraid to touch what they had claimed. And the mountain rose above them, magic flowing wraith-like down its shoulders. Men and women found each other, reached through their webs of sleep and opened like gifts under the strange spell of the land. In the morning they remembered nothing but visions of sweeping over the lagoon with the freedom of birds.

Along with the seed sown in the women, these dreams took root in Tumuital's mind. He came to expect them, curving above waves near enough to touch. But the land in these visions was different again from the mountain; night travel brought him outside the lagoon over water deeper than sleep, over the atoll of his grandfather and grandmother's birth. Waking, he knew his travels had not ceased. He might have reclaimed the mountain, but its magic had reclaimed him as well.

Origin

Of course it was Tonoken who paddled with him to the ringing reef at the edge of their fragile world. And it was Tonoken who braved the deep water between them and the atoll lurking southward. The clan had begged them not to go. Their wives had held children up like offerings so they would be powerless to leave, to no avail. Their shared legend drew them on like the lost children they were.

The atoll was ten miles away, its northern pass two hundred feet wide between island wall and reef. At its centre was a huge mound of coral rising toward the surface like a near-discovered secret. As the current drew them in, barracuda gleamed in silver schools below. The few islands nearby were low and wooded, those to the south slightly higher, as though the earth were slanted beneath. Rain rinsed the men of salt as they wandered the beach where once two spirits had rediscovered themselves. The friends slept beneath a near-full moon, its beams glossing the water white. Once Tumuital heard the sound of faraway laughter. When he lifted his head he saw figures—all small but two—gliding over the sand like clouds across the moon.

"This is the second part of our heritage," said Tumuital the next morning. "Birth came here from the mountain, as did death. They are one and the same, and so shall be their names."

A feast awaited them on their return. The clan danced and thanked the mountain for bringing their leaders safely home.

After all had eaten their fill of fish and fruit, Tumuital retold the story of their creation and why the Kuop atoll would not be settled. Its sacred terrain became the place of ritual, a pilgrimage for those seeking history within themselves. When the clan's boys came of age they struck out for the atoll to sleep amidst the shadows of their creators who still danced nightly over the sand. The clan grew strong in body and spirit, but maintained a fearful respect for the mountain they slept beneath. Years slipped into others like waves and Tumuital's people were healthy, content. New families from Param began to follow their path, but the journey was harder than it had once been.

Storm Rising

The sons of Ungo had stripped Ulalu's reefs of fish. The island's soil was exhausted, and the lone spring dried to a trickle. Ungoans worshipped the frigate bird; manhood on Ulalu was more a case of cleverness than strength. Men proved themselves through what they stole, especially power, and leadership was in constant flux. Small parties began leaving under a shared spell for theft. Eventually their clan rejoined on the long island of Fefan, but not before years of ever-moving and marauding among other clans. Their war parties worked best at night. With darkness their cloak, the most skilled were never seen; missing goods and slit throats were the only signs of their visitation. All paddling was done at night so no one knew their number, the exception being when travellers strayed between Tonoas and Fefan. Then the cruelly carved canoes of the Fefanites were seen and rarely escaped. After capture, no outsider was allowed off the island.

Women became wives or concubines; the men were publicly clubbed to death.

Tumuital knew the stories well. He had always feared the day when the clans of Ungo and Salat would fight. He preached for peace but readied for war. His men grew strong in arm, their feet light from foot-fighting. But as Tumuital neared eighty, the only sign he'd seen of their enemy across the water was the smoke of field fires and the few tales from those who had slipped through Fefan's nets to safety.

Fein

One morning a lone canoe washed up on the village beach, the boy inside nearly dead from blows and coral scrapes. Fein was sixteen with sunken cheeks and eyes that would not rest, even as they nursed him back to health. He and his brother had begun their voyage from Tsis in hope of joining the Salat clan through marriage, and had been set upon by marauders. His brother was dead from a spear point, Fein said; he had escaped by swimming through the surf of an isolated reef. The Fefanites could not follow in their canoes, and although injured, Fein had been able to save his dugout, which washed ashore. As the tide rose to his knees he had used driftwood and sharp coral to fashion a crude paddle and had fought his way out through the surf. He had almost reached Kuop when he fainted from blood loss.

Tumuital listened to the story carefully, then ordered that a hut be given to Fein at the edge of the village. Quietly, he ordered that no tools be allowed in the hut, and that no weapon be left unattended. Fein had been with them for nine days when screams woke the peaceful village from slumber. Tonoken lay on his mattress of fern, two sharp, segmented sticks thrust into his heart. They were love sticks, the ceremonial tools used when suitors came to call. The serrated wood could be slipped through the woven walls; asleep in her family's hut, a young woman would feel a love stick tangle in her hair and would know her suitor by telltale carvings. The night before the murder, Fein had admitted to Tumuital's wife, Utityu, his love for one of the village girls. He had begged her for the sticks so that he might try his fortune; she had yielded. Tonoken's own wife had died years before. He slept alone in a hut out at the farthest reach of the village. When his youngest daughter found him, her screams sang their tragedy.

Smoke

The day after the body was found, Tumuital set out over the water with his strongest warriors in their swiftest canoes. They carried provisions, spears and Tonoken's pandanus-swathed body. As the canoes slipped between Fefan and Tonoas, Tumuital stared out over the water toward Fefan's green coastline, but they navigated the pass without incident, and reached Moen by sunset. The next morning Tonoken was buried on the lookout point of the mountain his friend had once claimed for him. When they re-entered the pass, again Fefan's shores remained lifeless. The burial party was a mile from Kuop when Tumuital first saw the smoke, curling toward the heights of the mountain. Their strokes quickened, fears burning like the fires consuming their village huts. Drawing near, they saw no war canoes or evidence of battle, just smouldering ash and the odd lick of flames from what remained of their homes. They were still two canoe lengths from shore when the water around them erupted.

The ambushers had hidden in the shallows, breathing through hollowed reeds, their bodies weighted down with rock. Tumuital's men fought bravely, but were hopelessly outnumbered. Though old, Tumuital dispatched three of the enemy before spotting Fein on shore. For a moment they studied each other, then the boy turned and raced into the trees. With a scream, Tumuital charged from the water. He felt fern brush his skin, a still-flaming hut singe him as he closed in for the kill. But when Fein reached the centre of the village he turned to watch his brothers leap from hiding and strike.

FIRE

The marauders had come as they always did: at night, silently. Fein rode in the lead canoe, caressing his spear like a lover. From a young age, Fein had known he was different. His cruelty was not learned: it came from somewhere deeper, a pent-up hatred ever burning. He joined the raiding parties at age eight, scouting villages; judging size, potential risk. He planned his first raid at thirteen, forgoing stealth for diversion. Fire was his tool, and he used it well. Whether to lure warriors into ambushes or to flush prisoners from hiding, his calculated assaults left few villages standing. There were twice as many women on Fefan as men, living proof of his catch-all attacks. By fifteen he had fathered four children from different wives. Two had tried killing him in his sleep, but there were always more to replace them. He had already sized up Kuop's women; Fein's selections were earmarked, and any man who touched them chanced death. But it was not the women he wanted, not really. Great-great-grandfather Ungo's unanswered want of vengeance lived within Fein like a challenge, and one he felt destined to answer this very night.

His raiders anchored their canoes offshore, their footprints swept away with palm fronds so no sign remained of their landing. Stealthily, they fanned out through the sleeping village, each man assigned his partner and position. Once they were in place, Fein strolled casually into the village. But for one woman tending a fire in the circle's centre, all were asleep. She peered at him, not believing her eyes as, with a twisted smile, he stopped, tilted back his head and released a scream of such pained fury that Salat's clan scrambled from their huts. The slaughter was over in seconds; capture took longer. As the last old men and boys were dispatched, women rushed toward the beach to find their canoes gone, the paths guarded. Those who made for the trees had a better chance, but the thought of no escape was as effective a weapon as ambush for the men of Fefan.

Utityu's Quest

Utityu had slept poorly all night. After tossing and turning for hours on her fern bed, she crept to her daughter's hut and curled in the empty space beside Piaanu and her sleeping infant. Farada, Piaanu's husband, was the strongest warrior in the village: this is what saved them. Fein knew Farada would have gone to Moen with Tumuital, thus he wasted no men to guard a hut of women. At the sound of Fein's scream, Utityu pulled Piaanu to her feet, lifted her granddaughter to her breast, wrapped her in pandanus and was outside before the next breath escaped her. Shadows, screams flirted with darkness. She crashed through the underbrush with no real direction but *away*, Piaanu close on her heels. They could not escape by canoe; Utityu knew instinctively the beach would be guarded. The farther they fled into the jungle, the more certain she became that there *was* no escape. The stories of Fefan swept through her mind: rape, slavery, death. Tumuital would return to his destruction, and she had no way to save him.

They pushed on through eucalyptus and palm, finally reaching a moonlit stretch of sand. Piaanu wept quietly as Utityu turned and faced the mountain, their Creator, their supposed protector. Then she laid the child gently down and began gathering fronds from the fringing palms.

"What are you doing?" Piaanu asked between sobs.

"They may take us, but they will not take her. *Weave*, girl!" She pushed fronds into her daughter's arms. The strength in her voice surprised her and scared Piaanu even more. They sat for nearly an hour, their hands moving in silent counterpoint to the screams still audible from the village. Utityu took the woven fronds and connected them, shaping what looked like a cupped hand. Carefully she tore the pandanus sheet in half and used it as a lining. When satisfied, she placed the still sleeping child into the basket, tucked the rest of the pandanus around her and took the bundle down to the water's edge. Only when it touched wave did Piaanu scream and race after her mother.

"No, Mama, *she'll die!*"

Her mother turned and caught her, old arms filled with terrific strength.

"Better to die than face our sort of future!" She held her sobbing daughter close and watched the tide draw the bundle out to sea.

ADRIFT

Amidst the slaughter of that night, there was a strange occurrence. As the tide drew the bundle from shore, the sea calmed and a faint breeze picked up from the northwest. By daybreak the tiny craft had reached the perimeter reef; it slipped through a small channel and out. The wind built in strength. Waves steepened, grew longer, but the craft was so small that its delicate cargo was not threatened. The child's bright eyes watched patches of sky through the fronds and she gurgled in delight when the frigate bird circling above finally dove, stretched her claws and drew the craft up from the waves.

The load was heavier than the bird was used to, but frigates have a ruthlessly efficient design. Her wings were long and backswept, made for gliding and manoeuvres. The strange wind buoyed her aloft, and though tired when she reached her island, she knew the effort was worth the reward. With some adjustments the basket would make the perfect nest, all the more perfect because she had found it, not built it herself. But she was more tired than she knew. Cruising over surf and beach she misjudged her landing, and missed the crook of the eucalyptus that was her home. The basket clipped a branch, and she tumbled with a squawk into the foliage. The branches tore her wings as she tried to flap free. Had she let the basket fall she might have caught herself, but there was no way she would abandon what she had worked so hard for already.

Theirs was a rough, controlled fall to the forest floor. She knew her wing was broken even as her cargo began to scream. The frigate jumped away from the bundle, spreading her boomerang wings. Yes, one was definitely broken. But the bundle was broken too. The fall had not been serious, but the fronds had parted on one seam, and a fat pink claw gripped the air in frightened anger.

That is how Miaru found them: a girl-child in a woven basket, and a frigate with a broken wing. The infant seemed healthy, if angry, the bird angrier still. But Miaru's hands were both gentle and quick. She tucked the bird's head beneath one wing and bound her loosely with creeping vine. Miaru took the same vine and tied the basket to her back, then lifted the bird and strode off toward the village.

Mortlocks

The wing took a month to heal. The village chief named the frigate Ushi and saw that she received the best care possible. Her wing was splinted, and she was fed fish twice a day. Land was a new world for Ushi; it was strange to see these creatures without the vantage of height and speed. She was amazed by their hands. What marvellous things they could make, but what sort of motion was this, this rocking from one leg to the other? Their nakedness was equally perplexing; besides the shock of black on their beak-less heads, their feathers had been plucked. The child stayed in another hut nearby, but was brought to Ushi at intervals where they would rest under the same blanket. Ushi found herself preening the infant's silken locks, softer than any feather she knew.

This bond mystified the chief and Miaru both. The two spoke for hours at a time about the question of the infant's arrival and her relation to the bird, but as Ushi's bones knit the visits grew less frequent, their tone easier. In her final weeks before flying, Ushi spent a great deal of time out of doors. The chief would place her on his shoulder when he called his meetings. There were nearly six hundred citizens in all, and this led to both strength and disquiet. The chief had many opponents, but Ushi's dark presence on his shoulder unravelled them. For fun she even took to squawking when debate grew heated. Once her wing was fully healed Ushi did not return for weeks. The constant feeding at the village had made her fat. Rather than fishing she was content to glide on the updrafts and badger the terns returning from their day at sea. But Ushi's grounding had altered her, and though her own chicks and mates came and went she found herself drawn back over the village as though it too was a part of her territory, the dark, featherless child one of her own.

Suitors

Taualap grew quickly, her features strong but sensuous, hair long and black as tail feathers. She would turn and look whenever the bird swung out on updrafts over the village, never beckoning but glad when Ushi curved down to land on her shoulder. The young men were lured but alarmed by this; there seemed much magic in her, and Ushi's presence unmanned them.

Besides the chief, perhaps the only one unafraid of the frigate was Eo, the chief's second son. It was he who had fashioned the splint for Ushi's wing, and he who had made sure the bird received her daily rations during that long month on land. Unlike his father and elder brother, Eo was a thin boy with bones long and frail. He had spent many hours with Ushi, holding her gently in his hands, his brilliant eyes staring into her yellow ones as though mapping her thoughts. Ignoring his brother Hacq's mocking laugh, Eo kept the feathers she shed in a carved box by his mat. He even began wearing them in his hair as he grew older. His peers found him strange. Eo spent days in the jungle alone or, stranger still, with Otta, the lunatic witch who lived in the cave past the hill. Apart from her, Taualap was the only one he would talk to, and theirs were odd conversations. They spoke as though dreaming, their words disconnected, thoughts formed through image in the eye of the mind. But as Taualap grew older, the men around her grew bolder. Her beauty drowned their fear, and soon the contests began. The clansmen cheered as suitors wrestled in the centre of the village, and Eo watched in quiet fury as one after another fell before his brother Hacq's stony assault. Taualap and Hacq had been united a week when Eo took his herbs, roots and few other belongings over the hill.

Hacq's Burden

That Taualap bore him only one child caused Hacq much embarrassment. No one doubted his strength in combat, but he feared his enemies questioned his manhood. He tried every medicine available. He even went to Otta the witch, but her remedies did nothing. As a last resort he visited his estranged brother for a cure.

Eo squatted by his fire for some time before speaking.

"Is your son not enough? Is he not healthy and strong?"

"He is strong, but only one. A man needs children to bring strength to the clan, to help him in age . . ."

". . . and in status," Eo finished. He reached for a small earthen bowl, and took herbs from a basket and coals from the fire. All three met together under his deep-set eyes, and the herbs burned slowly in the bowl with a small curl of smoke. His long yellow fingernail moved for a time through the ash, then he looked sharply up at his brother.

"You should be happy, Hacq. What you have is rare and stronger than you think."

Only after Hacq left did the frigate hop back to Eo's shoulder from her hidden perch in the trees. Eo ran his fingers over her head, down the jet-black folds of her wings.

"You have lived long, Ushi. You have seen many things but will see more."

Fish-Fighting

Hacq's son, Sowukachaw, grew quick and strong. His build was slimmer than his father's but carried his strength, and he wore his mother's shroud of mystery. Hacq taught him to fish and to fight, but it was the hours spent with Taualap that the boy loved most. They would walk the beaches and climb into the hills to look out over the waves that stretched to the horizon. Sowukachaw never asked why she brought him there, nor would she have told him in those early years. But one afternoon down by the water brought questions worming into his mind.

The village boys had a favourite game: after digging a pool in the sand, they would catch fish in small nets, choose one each and make them fight. The other boys did not like Sowukachaw; he was quiet and strange, and in their fighting games moved with guile that rendered them helpless. Even the fish he championed always won. He had followed them this day as on others, and ignored the jibes that were meant to scare him off. When the fish he chose again beat all comers, they grew angry and cruel.

"It does not matter that you win. You're a foreigner, a freak! You don't belong here. You're not one of us!" Then, as though of one mind, they fell upon him, tearing at skin and hair. When he broke free and ran they laughed. One boy even grabbed his fish from the pool, screamed and tore it in half.

Taualap was not in the hut, and Hacq had not seen her for hours. He did see the tears and marks on his son.

"A man does not cry, Sowukachaw. Even in torture, they must not see your weakness."

The boy stood trembling, then ran from the hut. He had no real direction. Then the old bird gliding above caught his eye, as she wheeled high over the lookout. The boy did not check his speed; his feet knew where to fall on the twisting path. He was out of breath when he found his mother, Ushi perched in her hands. Taualap held him until he could speak, and wiped his face free of tears.

"They are wrong and right, my son. This is your home and it is not, and where you will go I cannot see. But come. Come with me."

She led him back down the path, but took a different turn at the bottom of the hill. They walked for some time through the forest, the narrow trail faint, overgrown. Finally they reached a clearing at the foot of the island's sole mountain. A small hut stood alone, the fire out front still smoking. Ushi alighted on a branch, its wood worn smooth already from her claws. Taualap bade Sowukachaw sit, then entered the hut, reappearing moments later with a strange figure in tow. The man was tall and heavily scarred with curious designs. His limbs were willowy and feathers adorned his long black hair. *He moves like smoke,* the boy thought as Eo settled down beside him.

Wordlessly, Eo prodded the fire's embers with a stick, then reached into one of the bowls scattered around the firepit for leaves to throw onto the coals. There was no wind, but the smoke curled toward the boy now anchored by his mother behind him. To Sowukachaw, Eo's voice was less sound than dreams pushing into his mind, seeping into his soul along with the smoke coiling snakelike around him.

"You've come a long way, my son, and will go farther. See your path, and remember."

The smoke thickened, drew around him like a cloak. When Eo added a black feather to the flames, the boy's eyes flickered shut.

First was sky, then water. Its expanse unrolled in waves longer than life, and he rolled with them. Islands grew from shadow to form, low at first, then high on the horizon. Before them, a reef stretched away, three low islands guarding a narrow pass. And sound, not of paddles, but a strange rhythmical creak: wood upon wood. Later Sowukachaw told his mother he had been flying on the water, neither bird nor dolphin, but something between. Inside the reef the islands were brooding and strange. All passed behind him but one. Its mountain was smooth and green, drawing him near as the sun rose and fell in one long arc of passage. At the mountain's foot he saw strange men moving around, their bodies hard and angular. The land hated them. Great patches of forest lay black and bare, like the bruises on the skin of the women who toiled despondently at their chores. Always smoke in the trees, over the roofs of the huts, curling in plumes toward the peak of the mountain. But never laughter. No, never that.

When his eyes opened they brimmed with tears. Sowukachaw had never seen these islands but knew them, and the tortured women seemed as familiar as the arms of his mother wrapped around him. He laid his head back against her breast.

"Have you seen it?" he whispered.

"No, son. But it is there. My home, and yours."

"How far?"

Taualap smiled inwardly. "Only Ushi knows for sure. Come. We must be back before dark."

She said nothing to Eo as they stood, but circling behind, her hand brushed his knotted hair gently. Eo sat staring into the fire a long time after they had gone. Finally Ushi spread her wings and landed heavily on his shoulder. He gave a start, saw the sun had set and began preparing their meal.

Predestination

There is great difference between a boy with purpose and one without. That night Sowukachaw dreamed again of the mountain he had seen through the smoke; by morning he knew he would claim the island for his own. The other boys were right to say he was not one of them, Sowukachaw thought. He was beyond them, and they would soon learn why.

Days later he found the first of his tormentors alone, fishing for bait for his father. Sowukachaw struck silently, pinning his prey helpless, hands tight around the boy's slim throat. He pressed slowly, let his prey feel life seep out with the last breath from his lungs. And then Sowukachaw released him, stood and vanished into the forest as his victim lay gasping.

Forewarned, the other boys were more careful. They moved in a pack, and stayed indoors when darkness fell. Sowukachaw waited them out. Eventually each boy fell the same way, tasting fear and mercy like the rest. The day after the last one was punished, Sowukachaw found them together on the beach. He walked slowly nearer as they fanned out, all five boys tensing for attack. A few carried spears, others picked up rocks from the sand. Sowukachaw carried nothing but a great frond-woven basket. When he was finally among them, he dropped his load at their feet, turned and walked away.

The fish inside were large and silver-grey blue. Such tuna only swam outside the reef where the sharks lurked; they were not hard to hook but nearly impossible to spear. There were five of them, each with a neat hole behind the gill plate, right through the heart. The boys studied this offering for some time as Sowukachaw slipped back into the trees.

Leader

Sowukachaw's rise began slowly, like most things that endure. The tale of the fish became known to all, and though never boasting he performed more feats of daring with ease. He was also a born leader. His hand was open to all; he taught by example, gave friendship willingly, yet commanded a fearful respect. By the age of eighteen he had organized a subclan, bound not by relations but young men's need for purpose—a dream to follow, to build upon. His past enemies were now his captains; with his father's skills he made them warriors.

Soon enough, the island's elders took notice. What was this strange organization, they demanded. How were they to maintain order if the youngest and strongest followed one with no fixed loyalties? But their fears fell on deaf ears. The old chief knew too well the influence of Sowukachaw's clan. The presence of these young warriors sitting behind him at council meetings had more effect than fifty frigate birds. Tensions had eased in the districts now that the troubled youth had purpose, and the chief's opponents were afraid of this new strength. Sowukachaw's clan was young, but fought with ruthless intelligence. And they were unafraid of the deep water. The chief's power now reached past his shores of Satowan, carried first by Sowukachaw's canoes, then, like a miracle, by wind.

Water and Wing

Sowukachaw had many dreams of the mountain. He knew the island like home, but each morning he puzzled over the creak of wood on wood and wind. He spent long hours at his lookout, watching birds riding updrafts, the dolphins playing below. *Like flying through water, between dolphin and bird.* One morning he was fishing with Uijec, his closest aide. They floated beyond the reef, their pandanus lines set deep. Hearing a splash behind him, Sowukachaw turned to see a tern surface with a needle fish in its bill. When the fish slipped free, the bird rolled and snatched it back from the waves, one wing still extended, buffeted by wind. Wordlessly Sowukachaw pulled up his line. Uijec did the same, and they paddled hard for shore. After beaching the canoe, Sowukachaw strode to the village and disappeared into his hut, returning with two fishing spears and his pandanus sleeping mat. Back at the beach he broke a spear over his knee and wove the equal sections into the mat, one on each end. He took the other spear and did the same up one side, then jammed its point into the sand, his body tense, waiting. The afternoon was calm, but a lone gust off the water caught the mat and spun it on its spear.

"What? What is it?" his friend demanded, unable to control himself any longer.

Sowukachaw said nothing. He just smiled and watched his sail tack in the breeze.

DEPARTURE

They left at dawn, 330 men on twenty-two boats. The craft were massive, with low huts on the platforms stretched between their twin hulls. The sails were triangles of woven pandanus hung on a single mast with a thick boom and lighter gaff suspending the top of the sail. For five summers Sowukachaw had experimented with different rigs on the short stretches of water between the surrounding islands. Off the stern of each boat was a huge wooden oar to steer by. Thick binds of pandanus attached the shaft to a crossbeam, and rigging stretched from the masthead fore and aft and to each side amidship.

The feast the night before had been bittersweet. He had spent quiet hours with his mother at the lookout, sitting in their familiar silence.

"You could come with us."

She shook her head, the ghost of a smile on her still-beautiful face.

"When we are victorious, I will send for you."

"Yes," she said.

He left her and moved down through the woods along the narrow trail to the village.

A nervous energy had infected the place. Voices were louder, men and boys pushed and played, laughing in the face of the unknown ahead. Uijec spied his leader and strode over.

"The chief awaits you in his hut."

Sowukachaw nodded and ducked inside.

When he first caught wind of Sowukachaw's plan, the old man had been furious. Now he sat stoically as his young protêgê settled on the mat before him.

"How will you find it, Sowukachaw, even if it is there?"

"It is there, Grandfather. My path may not be easy, but it *will be*."

"And when you find it?" the old man asked.

"War."

"With all this *peace* you have preached of."

"One before the other, Grandfather."

"And after, if you live? Will you return?"

Sowukachaw paused, his eyes focused far away suddenly, his voice gentle.

"Some may, but I will not. It is my home. I know this without knowing why . . . have known it since I was a boy."

"You are still a boy."

Sowukachaw smiled faintly. "And will be to you always. But I am a man to the others. We must go. They demand it."

The chief smashed his fist into his palm. "Only because you made them hunger for it with . . . with your sails and your mountains!"

"The curse of the young, Grandfather. Do you remember?"

The old man looked away. "I would have given you my chiefdom," he said softly.

Sowukachaw lifted his gaze.

"We will go with your blessing or not, Grandfather. But it is your blessing we want. On such a voyage as this we will need all the prayers we can get."

The old man regarded him silently for a moment, then nodded. Watching the sails reach for the horizon the next morning, he felt an ache he had never known and would later try to forget.

CROSSING

For days they sailed beneath sun and sky. The gaiety of departure swiftly gave way to quiet. Soon the only sounds were the hiss of the water, and the creak of the rigging and the oar in its mount. Sowukachaw spent most of his time under the canopy's cover, but at dawn and dusk he would rise and set a new course by the sun and the remembered bearing of a long-dreamed-of place.

Still no islands appeared. The grumblings of the men grew louder as their stores of taro grew spare. They had expected more fish, but had never been so far from land. Their catch was either the small bone-ridden flying fish or huge tuna that tore their lines to shreds. After the fifth day without success Sowukachaw bade them bait a hook with flying fish on a short line. An hour passed, then Uijec cried out.

Fifty yards behind, a flash of silver-green drove toward them so fast that it broke the top of each swell before punching into the next. Sowukachaw had his men bring the bait closer. The fish was almost upon them, the blunt hatchet-head of the *mahi mahi* visible as it closed. Their bait spun enticingly behind their starboard hull, but for a moment, the fish hesitated. Hunger made it bold, however, and as the *mahi mahi* charged Sowukachaw drove a spear through the wave and the fish's small heart. Stricken, it veered sharply and tore the spear from his hand, but he had fastened spare line to the shaft. His men cheered as they hoisted his kill aboard, their faith in their leader rekindled. Yet it was only one fish, and faith is a fickle beast at sea. By the next night the silence was again heavy, with still no sign of land. In the dark, squalls ripped into the rigging with shrieking gusts, hammered them with rain. Fresh water was a blessing, but three boats had vanished by morning. Sowukachaw shouldered his men's fear in silence, his dreams haunted by mutiny.

At dawn of the eighth day, Uijec called his leader out on deck. Sowukachaw took a long time to appear. He had not dreamed the night before, of the mountain or anything else. When he climbed out and saw the same unbroken span of water, despair almost swamped him.

"Nothing," he said bitterly.

"Look again," said Uijec.

Only then did Sowukachaw see her, a small black spot before the brightness of dawn. The first beams of morning hit just as Ushi overtook them, circled, then cruised off to the south. They changed course to follow, the prevailing wind pushing them on. Late the next afternoon they reached the reef that was the main lagoon's northeast edge. They caught fish in the pass, and put ashore on a sentinel island before the sun fell again. Sowukachaw let his men rest for several days, feasting on coconut and the familiar reef fish near land. But he did not celebrate. He spent his time in silence by the shore, studying the brooding darkness of land to the southwest. On the fifth night he gathered his men together before a huge bonfire.

"We have come far. You have seen what was dreamed, and now know it to be true. Prepare for the rest: the peace and the war."

They left before dawn, and were well under way as light fringed the dark bowl above them. As they paddled between Tonoas and Fefan, they saw smoke over the trees, that was all. Ahead, the mountain rose and seemed to sing in their hearts. Sowukachaw stayed in the bow with Ushi on his shoulder, touching her feathers in this now-waking dream. They anchored off Eten, a few miles northeast of their goal. There were inhabitants on the island, but they remained hidden, and Sowukachaw bade his men let them be.

The morning brought clouds; a flat glare lit the waters and the mountain so near. Sowukachaw's men tacked off Kuop's western shore as though testing the water. The villages visible were empty, but the forest had eyes. Only when the sun had reached its zenith did they make for the beach. Still a boat's length away, the forest erupted, spears flying like birds from the palms. Sowukachaw's men raised their new wooden shields and hauled hard on the anchor lines trailing overboard. Swiftly, their boats drew them back out to sea. As the angry defenders surged after them into the waves, Sowukachaw watched his own men burst from the trees behind them.

The night before, Uijec had led twelve boats to land in secret on Kuop's eastern shore. The Fefanites were raiders, not used to defence, and Fein, their shrewdest leader, had died years ago. The Fefanites had seen Sowukachaw's party land at Eten, and no provision had been made for anything but frontal assault. When 180 warriors appeared from behind them, the Fefanites fled and they died. Sowukachaw's boats surged back to shore, adding spears to the rout.

Piaanu's Tale

Sowukachaw's men still guarded the coast, both to mop up any Fefanites still lurking and to watch for counterattack. With the women and children gathered together Sowukachaw told them stories of his dream, their passage, and the rule he envisioned. He knew their plight, how they had been taken, enslaved. They could stay and build if they wished, but any who chose to leave were free to go. Some did, paddling the same canoes that had captured them months or years ago. But many stayed: the old and the young who knew no other home, and their mothers who studied the liberators with more than idle curiosity. The woman who came to Sowukachaw's hut was ancient, her skin creased from hardship, but he welcomed her warmly.

"Have you been treated well, old mother?" he asked as she sat.

"Well enough." She studied him closely, her eyes like a bird's. "You have come a long way for a dream. Is it as you hoped?"

He smiled, chose his words carefully.

"I find it less and more. Is that a fair enough answer? I have dreamed of this place since I was a boy. I know now I came for answers, but they may not be here."

"Tell me these dreams," she commanded.

The small hut seemed to swell as words rolled from him.

"And your mother? Where is she?" The woman's body was stiff, her muscles tense under wrinkled skin.

He shrugged.

"Behind me. She claimed one voyage was enough. That this place did not live for her in dreams, that Satowan was home." He looked closely and saw tears welling in her eyes. "What? What is it, mother?"

"She knows less than she thinks. She should have come home . . . come home to *me*."

Sowukachaw said nothing, and her words spilled over the floor, swept him up in a torrent like a flood from the sky. He heard the screams in darkness, ran with her mother and his through the trees, saw the lone stretch of beach where Taualap had been left for the waves to save. He saw the battle that followed, her helplessness as Tumuital died. But that was far from all. This old woman spoke of her mother, Utityu, how after freeing the child they had ascended the heights of the mountain to live in caves, even in trees to avoid capture. They watched the bodies of their men thrown into the water for the sharks, saw Tumuital's corpse wash back on the reef. It was Utityu who had pulled him back to shore and rescued an abandoned canoe. Under cover, in constant fear of capture, they fashioned rough paddles and slipped away with the body at nightfall, heading south. They rested for some days on a small perimeter island, eyeing Kuop's atoll on the horizon. They paddled for hours, her mother's strength pushing them on, and the next day, his corpse weighed with stone, Tumuital was buried on the sunken reef in the middle of Kuop's pass. Piaanu's trials were not over, however. Utityu's fire drowned with her husband. Piaanu buried her days later in the same soil where generations ago spirits had played without fear.

"I walked alone for weeks, feeding on coconut and crab, my spirit broken, the shade of a soul. I was so glad to see them when the canoes arrived. . . ."

Piaanu had been the sole prisoner from Fein's scouting run. He had taken her back, then took her with the other women he had marked for his own. And she bent to him, toiled with the rest under his new harsh rule. There were times when she wished to die, to throw herself on a spear. Only the thought of her child floating forever at sea kept her alive. The torture of not knowing had cursed her with the life she endured.

As her tale unfolded Sowukachaw moved closer, drawn by her words. When she finished he took her in his arms, his only wish to ease her pain's release.

Ushi's Flight

Sowukachaw did not return with the boats that sailed that spring. He did send word that Taualap should come when the winds turned again, but a year later she still had not arrived. She is ill, his captains reported; she would never survive the passage. When next the sails grew over the horizon they told him she was dying. Sowukachaw took the news silently. He climbed alone up the mountain to look over his land, the islands and waves he had mastered. *She should be here,* he thought. *This is her place more than my own.* He sat there for hours, his mood as black as the shadow curving through the air toward him.

Ushi had flown so many miles that she was lost in them. She yearned to die, but did not know how. It was as though some unseen force had breathed life into her bones for a purpose she could not fathom. Cataracts clouded her once-brilliant eyes. Her feathers were tattered, and wing muscles groaned on the wind that would not free her. Below, the clan worshipped her form. She wished they would stop, thinking perhaps this homage denied release from her days of endless gliding. Seeing Sowukachaw through her misted vision, Ushi fell into his hands like an offering, hoping he might know some way to release her.

He caressed her fragile skull and his fingers drifted through her feathers, his voice soft in her ear.

"One last flight, Ushi, one last thing for you to do. You carried her once. Leave her shell, but bring her soul to the cradle. You will know how."

Passage

Eo moved around his hut like a ghost. They had brought Taualap to him days before. Looking into his brother Hacq's eyes, Eo knew he was leaving her to die. He felt a flicker of sympathy for Hacq then, at this strong man abandoned, warmed only by muscle and his need to prove himself. *Age will treat him harshly*, Eo thought, but such was the way of things. As Hacq disappeared down the path, Eo stoked the fire and turned to Taualap, to her all-consuming illness.

There was some improvement at first: his herbs and roots cleansed the toxins from her shrunken body. She began eating, and slept a few hours at a time. Remission was short-lived, however. Soon she grew weaker, her clear moments more fleeting. The harder he strove for a cure, the more certain Eo became that her sickness was of the soul, a longing so great that his charms were powerless. Finally all he could do was make her as comfortable as possible, and show she was not alone. She withered before his eyes, her face still beautiful, but ancient. In her few lucid moments, all she could speak of were dreams of gliding across water. On the last day she slept well into the afternoon, waking slowly, her eyes brilliant when they opened.

"Take me to the lookout. Please, it is time."

As always, he could do nothing but obey. The climb up the path was long, but she was so light in sickness that he had no difficulty carrying her. Beyond the lookout, the sky stretched away, sun tinting the waves amber. Eo placed Taualap down gently.

"There," she breathed, her wasted arm struggling to point.

The bird came in low, almost touching the water. Then an updraft from the beach swept her up, over the trees in one rising arc. Eo had not seen the frigate in years, but was as sure it was Ushi as he was that the sun would rise anew. Behind him, Taualap pushed herself to her knees, opening her arms wide, eyes closed. The bird's shadow crossed her own and drew her back over the waves, her body a husk left below where Eo roared, exalted.

Return

Wind welcomed them, carried them faster than thought. Their two wings were strong again, their yellow eyes clear. They chased the light fading west, and flew as one over Kuop's pass where her grandfather slept, past the sand where all began. Touching the horizon, the sun was on fire, its light singeing their wings, setting them ablaze. From the foot of the mountain Kuop's people watched them brilliantly burn. They fell with glorious light, and their flame struck the world with force greater than any thunder. For days a glow hung over the atoll, but, like all things, it faded, its brilliance but a memory now, alive only in song, colours lost and found in the slow whirlwind of time.

HUNGA PASS

Toa Falesi sat on the launch's port rail, his broad feet resting on a case of dynamite that lay on the pitching deck. This was not just reckless posturing, though the others—the Governor of Vava'u included—were duly impressed. Since being contracted to deepen the pass, Toa had developed a maternal apprehension about this crate, and rightly so, he thought. After all, *he* had examined the site with mask and snorkel. He had gone to the Australian Consul in Nuku'alofa to request the dynamite and fuses. And it was on him alone that responsibility rested: the Governor had made that perfectly clear. Only pride eased the stress Toa was under, the pride of having such an important duty at so young an age. After all, was his village not preparing a feast in his honour? It was. And what was more, the Governor himself—this massive near noble braying with laughter at Lotu's dirty jokes—was to preside over the celebration! Toa grinned to himself. This was a proud day for the Falesi family, a fact his elder brothers could not deny. He recalled the parting words of his sponsors in America, about his becoming a tool of progress, and grinned even wider. Yes, he was bringing the message, and in a way most would see as miraculous. Toa rubbed his bare soles against the crate like a hen checking her clutch: potent, fragile with potential.

Near the bow of the launch, Vava'u's Governor lit a French cigarette and studied Toa from the corner of his eye. The boy was frail by Tongan standards and betrayed quick birdlike movements the Governor did not trust. Only after much pressure from the palace had he conceded that Toa should lead the operation. The Governor's knowledge of local families was legendary—indeed, this very reputation had secured his official position—and the more he learned about Toa the less he liked. *Fakaleiti* or not, Toa had been a strange child, a loner who not only attended classes regularly but actually learned what his tutors found time to teach. When Toa graduated from high school, his family turned Mormon so the boy could attend college in America. Add to this the fact that his father, Semisi, made monthly pilgrimages seeking permission to expand his landholdings . . . Ambition would lead to arrogance, which could threaten all the bureaucratic harmony the Governor had taken such pains to achieve.

The Governor knew nothing about blasting, but he knew his people. In the minds of modern Tongans, *buho* was magic, and a man who could tame explosives was close to divine. They were already preparing a feast for the minnow back in Fungamisi, a celebration the Governor was not looking forward to. A free meal was one thing, a meal in someone else's honour quite another. But nothing could be done. No other Tongan knew about dynamite. All previous blasting had been done by the Americans, and the King demanded a homegrown example to front his new education program. The program would never last, thought the Governor, but this certainty did not help him now. He flicked his cigarette into the placid mouth of the Port of Refuge and watched Toa—not yet with fear, but with a gnawing apprehension.

The launch carved through the swells like a dolphin, rolling gently as Lotu turned them westward with the waves. The morning was calm, but far to the east he could see a long cloud bank approaching. *Never mind,* Lotu thought. Both outboards working was good omen enough. He brought the wheel to port and tucked up into Hunga Island's lee. On its northern end, Hunga looked like all islands in Vava'u: long and flat, swathed with a jungle of green. There was no beach; the last forty feet were sheer limestone dropping straight into the water. But Hunga's lagoon was unlike anything in the kingdom. Cliffs rose high on each side of the narrow entrance, and at mid-channel, a mushroom-shaped pinnacle jutted up ten feet. Another pass lay to the south, but it was long and too shallow to be of use for anything but dinghies. The western pass was ideal for blasting, its shallow zone only ten feet long. Toa figured one crate's worth of dynamite would do the job, and no one was in a position to argue. There were times he wished someone was.

Toa had never done underwater work. In fact, he had not done much above water, either. His expertise consisted of a Salt Lake City summer working for Utah's department of roads with Elvis, the demolition expert. Under his tutor's strange yellow-green gaze Toa had learned to drill holes for the charges, and link all the components together. Yes, he had handled dynamite, but as for heading his own operation, and *underwater* of all places . . . well, he had felt more comfortable in his life, truth be told.

His Mormon sponsors—or rather Mr. Tilley—had got him the job. An accountant for the department of roads, Charles Tilley had remained guarded during the first few weeks of Toa's stay. The boy was obviously bright and interested in learning, but . . .

"Don't you find him a bit, well, *queer?*" Tilley asked his wife one afternoon.

Deirdre Tilley looked quickly at her husband, a small man with a complexion ruddy enough to be suspicious given the Mormon rule of abstinence from alcohol.

"Of course Toa's different. What do you expect? Tonga might as well be another planet compared to this. He's very sweet. Instead of making fun of him you might just learn a few things!"

Tilley jerked back his head. "I wasn't making fun! All I meant was that he seemed a bit . . ." he paused, his best term spent already.

"Effeminate?"

"Exactly!"

She swivelled in her chair like a turret. "Did you by chance read any of the information the elders sent us?"

"'Course I did. You saw me."

"No, I saw you flip through the photo supplement and flake out on the couch."

"Well," he grumbled, "unless you can see through knitting magazines I didn't spot you doing much better."

Deirdre patted her greying coif. "Perhaps not, dear, but Toa and I *talk*. It might be an idea for you to look back over your notes on the *fakaleiti*."

"What's that, Tongan for fairy?"

"Charles!"

"He's got his ears pierced, Dee. He even brought me a skirt!"

"It's called a *lavalava*, and so what if he did? He can't help the way he was raised!"

Charles eyed her suspiciously. "What are you on about, woman?"

So she repeated what Toa had told her. How Tongan families with many boys and no girls often treated the youngest as female. How that child was raised to help with cooking, cleaning, tending the men. How it was natural enough in Tonga for these boys—these *leitis*—to acquire feminine characteristics until they left home and assumed regular male roles and mannerisms.

"So he's not gay?"

"You know the church's stance on that; they wouldn't have sent him if he was. Goodness, Charles. Sometimes I just don't know about you. What happened to *love thy neighbour?*"

She rose haughtily but on entering the sunlit kitchen her demeanour brightened. Toa sat with the cookbook she'd given him, legs crossed at the knees beneath a patterned brown *lavalava,* his fine brows knit in concentration. Sitting beside him, she again admired the waves of his lustrous black hair, the delicate slope of his neck and shoulders.

"How are things going, dear?"

"Good, Mrs. Tilley. But much is strange to me. I do not know many foods here."

"Well, Mr. Tilley and I both thought you did a wonderful job with dinner last night. The sweet potatoes were especially delicious."

Toa blushed deeply.

"What is *quiche?*"

"Oh, it's delicious. We use lots of eggs and cheese and vegetables like onions and peppers, then add whatever else we want, like spiced sausage or ham. You mix it all together and bake it. Like a pie, but different. I could show you if you'd like, after you've put the washing away."

"All done, but I left Mr. Tilley's in the basket." He added softly: "I don't think he likes me in his room."

Deirdre frowned and took his hand, thin-boned but toughened from years of housework.

"Nonsense. Charles was just telling me how happy he is that you're with us, and how helpful you've been."

Doubt clouded Toa's dark eyes.

"Oh, I know he doesn't say much, but Charles is very shy around young people. Not having children of our own makes it hard." She patted his hand. "Never you mind, dear. He'll loosen up. Just do as you've been doing, and I guarantee he will." Deirdre searched his slim face. She still saw doubt there, but less.

"You know, you have the most beautiful brows I've ever seen. Do you pluck them?"

Toa blushed again, and confided that no, they just grew that way.

"Well, they're lovely. I'm quite jealous, really. It makes me think of what I used to do as a girl to make myself handsome. In fact, I have some old things hanging around in the attic in case I ever had a daught—a child of my own. Let's get that washing away and see what we can find for you." She rose, then paused over the cookbook still lying open on the table. "Hmm. You'll try the quiche tonight, yes? I think I have everything you'll need."

"Would Mr. Tilley like it?"

Deirdre smiled. "Yes dear; I *know* he'll just love it."

THE FOLLOWING WEEK, CHARLES TOOK TOA to work with him. The road was slick with old rain and their tires hissed over the pavement. Driving gave Toa a curious sensation. Compared to Vava'u's rutted tracks these tarred roads were impossibly smooth. With the still-strange scenes of pristine houses and manicured lawns floating by, he felt caught in a waking dream.

"I really think you're going to enjoy this, Toa. I've talked to a friend of mine, Bill Hartley, and he's got a spot for you on the team resurfacing Clemons Road. Money's good for summer work; I know you'll want to send home what you don't use for school. Anyway, it'll be good for you. Get you out of the house, put some hair on your chest!"

Toa watched farms and fields whip past the car window. Tilley had given him some old work clothes to wear. The too-large pants bunched uncomfortably between his legs, and the T-shirt hugged tightly round his neck. Toa said nothing, however. He knew what was expected.

When he had grown old enough to learn why *leitis* were different, Toa had accepted his role without complaint. This was the way of things, his father told him. But only recently Semisi had shown Toa that roles were not immutable. To continue his studies Toa needed sponsorship, and the Mormons were the only ones who could pay. So the Falesis had turned Mormon, just like that. The change remained an incredible shock for Toa. He had gone to the Catholic church twice a week since before he could remember, been baptized and confirmed along with countless cousins by Father Uili. Then suddenly the Falesis walked a different road on Sunday, up the paved drive to the Mormon church whitewashed and perfect, crisp as a starched collar in the sun. It wasn't so bad, he supposed. Christ still died, they still consumed his flesh and blood with the Holy Sacrament, but . . . it was not just his new shirt and the name tag on its breast pocket that were different.

"Toa, it is important that you listen to me now. The people you are going to meet are good people, very important people for us. You are an intelligent boy and you deserve to go to college in America. The elders will see this, but . . ." Semisi paused, his expression like one with a lemon in his mouth. "People here understand about boys like you. But the people you will live with in America do not know about our ways. It is very important that you show them you can fit in with the people from America." He smiled expectantly, as though his meaning was perfectly clear.

"Fit in, Father?"

Semisi frowned. "Toa, you must show them that you are a regular boy."

"I am a regular boy."

He watched his father begin to pace.

"As a *fakaleiti* you are not a regular boy in America. It is very important to show these people that you can be a regular boy in America. Watch your brothers, the way they walk, the way they *sit*. You must act like them if you want to go to America. You do want to go to America, don't you? Of course you do! Think of what you will learn there! Think of the money you can make for your family, and the positions that will open to you when you return. It is very important that you do this, Toa. Do not disappoint me."

Regular or not, Toa was an intelligent boy. Instead of crying he slowly nodded his head and did what was asked. He altered how he walked and sat, pretending to be one of his stout, lazy brothers. He fixed himself rigidly in a chair before the committee, determined not to move, answering their questions with as few words as possible, terrified that even these might betray him and his family.

When Toa was awarded the scholarship, Semisi threw a feast in his honour. Such celebration had been Toa's sweetest fantasy, but any joy was replaced by unease. Perhaps the Mormons had sent someone to spy on him, to see who he *really* was. As guests laughed and danced to "Blue Suede Shoes" rewound again and again on the old cassette player, Toa sat watching from one corner, uncertain how to be. Then his life changed again, transported across the ocean to a land where only the words of a new religion were familiar. And now, he travelled by car over roads as smooth as a dream to be dropped into yet another realm, the man's world of sweat and dirt and leaning on shovels.

Toa did feel an undeniable excitement. To watch something grow day after day, progress marked in measured feet . . . He had seen other road crews during his first weeks in the country. He wondered how long before he would be driving a roller, or a backhoe even. The taunts of his older brothers washed over him like waves. *You can't run, you can't throw. Go help mama, little girl.* Toa cracked open the car window until the wind drowned out their voices. He wished to control something of his own for once, but when the crew foreman handed him the STOP/SLOW sign Toa could not even control his disappointment. He just slunk off to the outhouse and hoped his tears would stop before long.

TOA HAD WORKED THE ROAD for a week when Elvis appeared. The grind of the grader hid the noise of his speeding truck, but Toa, mind settling into its by-now-necessary numbness, spotted the red pickup a quarter mile off—disappearing, reappearing with each undulation of road. The closer the truck got, the more nervous Toa became; the chassis shook so badly it seemed possessed, and was steered with such genuine recklessness that he knew beyond doubt the driver was completely insane. With a squeal of tires the truck swerved left, then right, then shot by so close that its passage spun his sign from STOP to SLOW. Toa turned to see the truck pitch up on two wheels, then slew 180 degrees to park perfectly on the side of the road.

The man who got out had dark hair and sideburns framing a bland-featured face. He drew out and lit a cigarette with practised ease, inhaling so deeply the smoke never emerged. His sunglasses had thick silver frames with ever-shrinking circles cut out of the arms, their lenses square, brown-tinted but not quite opaque. He looked a bit over thirty until you saw his eyes: their irises seemed ancient, with green flecks set on a pale, pusy hue. But this Toa noticed only later. For the moment he stood frozen in the middle of the road. He was amazed to be alive, but even more amazed that he had not run, had not even flinched as death brushed past. Watching Elvis swagger over to the foreman, Toa realized that he felt strong, like a *man*.

The terrain had changed in the past few working days. There were still the same dilapidated cottages and smaller homes along the old gravel track, but the ground had grown uneven. Amidst boulders and limestone plates, the peaks and valleys of the road had assumed more severe angles. "Have to flatten that out," Matt, the foreman, said. Pavement meant speed; with those sorts of hills, cars would be flying off corners. Toa took his word for this. Nor did he ask why they were upgrading such a quiet road in the first place. It was enough just to see pavement laid, progress achieved.

On either shoulder, last night's rain dripped from forest to rock. The rain smell reminded Toa of home and the jungle; the washed-moss scent was gone by lunchtime, as was the red truck. With Matt in the passenger seat, Elvis had sped off, the Chevy leaping over crests like a gazelle. Toa sat with his lunch in the shadow of a roller as the other workmen talked among themselves. For once he knew they were not talking about him.

". . . the guy nearly bled to death, I heard."

"He's a fucking lunatic."

"Have to be to do that for a living."

"Ah, c'mon. S'not as dangerous as you think."

" 'Cept that one time it is."

In the lunch-break stillness all heard the truck returning. When it streaked over the last rise, Toa swore he saw all four wheels leave the road. The same sort of finale: a lean, a hard skid, then the tail slewing into a perfect parallel park. When the dust cleared Elvis stood hands on hips before them like some diminutive 1950s superhero. His coveralls were spotless and green, wide blue belt matching his slant-heeled eel-skin boots. Foreman Matt was still in the truck, head down, hands palming the dashboard like a gut-shot sprinter. Elvis drew a pack of Malls from his pocket, offered them out.

"How are ya, Nate? Your wife miss me? Looking trim as ever, Bud, ol' pal." A few took cigarettes, but grudgingly.

"Listen boys, it's your lucky day. I just been talking to Matty there about some blast work needs doing. My second, Gaines, is taking a holiday and I'm looking for a hand. Temporary-like, till he's back on his feet."

"From what I hear it was Gainesy's foot went kind of temporary."

Elvis took a haul from his cigarette. "Well, it's like that with kids. You teach 'em best you can, but they gotta learn the hard lessons themselves."

Toa dropped his lunch and edged toward the gathering. He had never heard the real Elvis speak, but there was something familiar in this man's velvet tremolo, in the dip of tone at the end of each line as if he were slipping down a sentence.

"Look," said Elvis, "it's easy enough for me to get new meat from the warehouse, but it's good pay and I thought one of you could use the green. And who knows, maybe pick up a skill while you're at it."

"How good is the pay?"

Elvis spun around sharply. "Who the hell're you?"

"Your fairy godmother," quipped Bud, and snickered with the rest.

Elvis pulled down his glasses and gave Toa the full attention of his weirdly coloured eyes.

"Where you from, boy?"

"Tonga."

". . . in the *Thouth Pathific*."

Elvis sucked his teeth noisily. "Easy, Wayne; that's cannibal country. Ever eat a man, son?"

Toa ignored his colleagues' grins and shook his head.

"How long you been working this road?"

"One week."

"Know anything 'bout explosives?"

"Nobel invented them."

Elvis laughed, a melodic staccato that rose, then fell into silence.

"Where you living?"

"With the Tilleys."

He gave Toa another hard look.

"You're the guy with the sign. I scare ya?"

Again Toa felt the truck brush past, felt the fear, the stab of joy a second later, and smiled.

Elvis pushed his glasses back up. "All right, wonder boy, you got yourself a job."

ONCE THROUGH THE PASS, Lotu cut the engines, ran forward and tossed the anchor over the bow. Toa began hauling in the small skiff they had trailed behind them, but there was no real need to hurry. Most resident Hungans were against the blasting, so to pacify them the Governor had hired two locals, and Toa could do little until they arrived. For the umpteenth time he checked his supply box: fuse, blasting caps, plunger. Toa decided not to open the dynamite until he was in position. Instead he asked Lotu to help him transfer the scuba tank and gear to the skiff. There was water in its bottom, which Toa bailed as dry as he could before moving forward to check the anchor line. A fishing boat approached from across the lagoon, the two men inside waving as though celebrating a catch. When it reached the government launch Toa ignored their friendly banter and reworked his plan one more time.

"The most important thing to remember is how sensitive the dynamite is. No one is to touch it but myself and Lotu. I will rig the charges at the surface before I go in, then have Lotu hand them over the side to me in the water. You, Fala, will hold on to the fuse while I place the charges. Don't worry, it won't be hooked up to the plunger until I'm aboard. Just hold the end so it doesn't get wet. Now you will control the anchor and line, and you, Ongo, will work the motor if we need to move the skiff. All right, the two of you get in with me. Fala, you and Lotu are to *carefully* pass over the crate once I'm in."

Toa stepped aboard the dinghy and made sure the Hungans were safely out of the way. The skiff was old and of local construction; flat-bottomed, it rocked with any shift in weight.

"Okay, Lotu. Hand it over."

Toa knew Fala and Lotu from childhood. Both were from the same village and both were fairly trustworthy. As the crate was passed Toa noticed the bottom corner looked damp, as if it had been smeared with Mrs. Tilley's apple jelly. He stowed it carefully under the slatted bench, then Lotu climbed in behind him and yanked the starter cord. The engine caught on the second try; Fala cast off their lines, jumped aboard, and they pulled away from the launch. *There are too many in the boat,* Toa thought, but said nothing. He was destined to do this thing. When he waved to the Governor, the Governor did not wave back.

They crept slowly into the throat of the pass. There was little swell but the line of cloud Lotu had noticed was drawing ominously over the northern rim of the island. Toa signalled to slow, then put his snorkel mask on and leaned over the side, looking for the marker he had left. Yes, there it was, a red rag waving gently on a stick jammed into the coral. He pulled his head back out of the water.

"Drop here."

Their hook plunged obediently overboard. Unfortunately, the Hungan named Ruto had been careless with his feet. The anchor was small but when its line looped one ankle he stumbled and fell. The last thing he remembered was the scuba tank rolling toward the crate.

NOT UNTIL HE FIRST SIZED UP Hunga Pass did Toa realize how little he had actually learned about blasting. The insight came as a complete shock to him. He had always been a gifted student; what he heard he quickly understood. But when he lay in bed at night sifting through his days with Elvis it was not facts and techniques he recalled but conversations, comments, his mentor's endless queries. And all recollection was surrounded by a strange, reeling confusion, as though body and mind were out of kilter.

In retrospect Toa saw that Elvis was a horrible teacher. He did not know why a charge placed here rather than there would be more effective, he just knew this was so. He was the same behind the wheel. If there were cars, Elvis passed them with manoeuvres demanding both nerve and a clairvoyant sense of what the other drivers would do. He had yet to kill anyone on the road for the same reason he had not killed himself through blasting: he was charmed. In Elvis's logic, over-thinking could only undermine the fact.

Toa had simply been along for the ride, and that summer was unlike any he had ever known. He was always off balance, braced for impact, but drunk with the thrill. There was no escape. Even Elvis's queries were like their first encounter: the truck bearing down on him, changing him forever.

Their second day together was a perfect example. Three miles' drive past the crew, a section of road coupled a sudden crest with a violent curve around a high rock outcropping. The crest would be smoothed with the grader once they blew off the edge of the ridge. After showing Toa how to use the coring drill, Elvis prepared the charge to drop down the hole.

"So what's the deal, kid? You queer or aren't cha?"

"Queer?"

"You like boys or girls?"

The morning was warm and beautifully quiet. Surrounded by the alien trees and undergrowth of an American forest Toa was suddenly tired of hiding, of trying to belong. He looked at the small strange man standing near him and shrugged. "I don't know."

"Well, why don't you know?"

Toa stared back, stunned. In eighteen years this was the first time anyone had asked *his* opinion. A flush of gratitude ran through him, then confusion. His mind spoke permutations, mechanics, lines and curves. Emotions were more foreign than English and suddenly he felt, well, *stupid*.

Elvis dropped the fuse and stepped toward him.

"Let me give you a hand, boy. You like when I do *this?*" He reached out and gave Toa's crotch a gentle squeeze.

Toa said nothing, he *did* nothing. His mind reeled as Elvis took his hand back, took a step back, and gazed sombrely through brown lenses.

"Yeah, you sure *are* screwed up."

Several minutes passed before Toa worked up his courage.

"Why did you do that?"

Elvis scratched one sideburn. "Had a question you couldn't answer and thought that might. Don't like suspense, you see. Gets me all *edgy*-like."

"Are *you?*"

"Edgy?"

"Queer."

"Why, wish I was?" he chuckled, wiring his fuse into the plunger box.

Toa was not laughing. Besides his parents, no one had ever touched him before, and certainly not in that way. His body still buzzed—not because the touch was intimate or male, but because it was contact.

"Maybe," said Toa slowly, "but just so you could tell me things."

Elvis sighed. "Son, I don't have to be a fag to tell you things. I can tell you all kinds of things you don't know. Like why we're building a nine-million-dollar road in the middle of nowhere. Like how yer pal Nate's wife's face screws up when she's coming, or what Foreman Matt really does when he says he's off hunting deer. I can tell ya what Mormons think of homos. I can even tell you how ol' Tilley's face got red, but I won't. You know why? Because the fun's finding out yerself. Me, I hate suspense, but I got a feeling *you* just love it." He gazed out from their vantage point of the ridge. "Not many things're as they seem in this world. It's all image, what we create. Only on the edge you find the true nature of things." He held up the plunger box and smiled. "Fear of death blows the face right fucking off."

This was a fairly small explosion, but limestone fell away as though sliced, the blown cliff bare as a new beginning.

THE SUMMER FLEW BY FOR TOA. At the Tilleys', things had settled into a comfortable routine. He saw himself as a tenant and did not mind playing the role. He woke early, and took care of his chores before making breakfast for himself and his sponsors. Then he was off, striding out to the main road where Elvis would come swooping over the hill in his truck like a demented angel. At work Toa took chances, and pushed Elvis further into recklessness. Finally, risk grew more important than learning, as though each brush with death proved what Toa had always known: that he too was charmed, meant for something more than his *fakaleiti* role. There were times when he longed for the rickety beams of his old home. At work in the Tilley kitchen, he would picture his mother among her battered pots, the yam boiling, the gas sputtering like an eternal flame. But the memory of those days filled him with weariness; the thought of his brothers, with dread. For years he had endured their abuse like a dog trading beatings for food. Half the reason he'd liked school was that it gave him a refuge where his tormentors seldom strayed. With Elvis, he had found another refuge. The other workmen still tossed insults when Toa was within range, but he knew that beneath them lay a rueful respect for one brave enough to work with a lunatic. He had never known respect at home. Soon Toa did not want to go home.

"It's natural enough, kid, but I doubt it'll last. Anyhoo, you *have* to go back, yeah?"

Toa nodded. To promote the Mormon cause in Tonga, his scholarship stipulated return.

Elvis reached behind the truck seat and grabbed a beer from the Styrofoam cooler.

"Well, I wouldn't worry too much. They may give you the same ol' shit, but you're different now. Make the best of it. Blow the fuckers away. Shit, I got half a mind ta come with ya and put my boot up the arse a' those brothers of yours. Teach 'em a lesson or two." Then he looked over and smiled. "But they'll get the message."

THEY COULD FEEL *BUHO* in the village, shaking the ground. The cloud rose high and grey as splinters scattered like leaves over the lagoon. Of the five in the boat, only the two Hungans flew up and landed in the water without a scratch. The other men were gone. When the Governor approached the village wharf to ask people for help, they shook their heads but still got into their boats to go looking. The parts they found were very small and because no one could tell who was who, the searchers made three piles, wrapped each one in tapa, and returned them to Neiafu for burial. Three days later a Hungan out fishing saw something floating in the water. Slowing his skiff, he poked it with an oar to discover a body with no arms or legs. But it was early in the day and he still wanted to fish. Rather than lift the body out he tied it with fishing line to a tree and fetched it when he returned. The next morning, Ruto identified the corpse and was told to take it back to Neiafu.

Ruto did not want to go, but there was no one else. The petrol barge was not due until the next day; everyone else had either used up their gas during the search or now used that excuse. And thanks to Ongo, everyone knew about the scuba tank. Much of the day was gone by the time he cast off. The tapa-wrapped corpse lay in the bow with a bottle of whisky to ease Ruto's guilt or the thirty-mile voyage or both. The swell rarely got big between islands, but built steep enough to make the ride uncomfortable. Beyond Hunga's protection, spray soaked through the tapa as the body rolled from side to side with each wave. Ruto crouched miserably in the stern and opened the whisky.

He reached the Neiafu wharf an hour before sunset. The waterfront was deserted but for a few children swimming, so Ruto sat on an old piling to wait. One of Toa's brothers was supposed to transport the body by truck to the family home in Fungamisi, but as the sun slipped behind the flat peak of Mount Talau, Ruto knew they had either forgotten or never been told. He was unsure what to do, only that he did not want the body in his boat. Such a thing was sure to bring bad luck; the sooner it was gone the better. He tipped more whisky down his throat, taking courage from its rugged warmth. Fungamisi was on the other side of the island, but the bay cut deep through the heart of Vava'u and had a small pass to the northeast shore. He knew Fungamisi well; a cousin lived there and Ruto had actually met

Semisi Falesi before. He studied the sky. Less than an hour of light left, and still no sign of anyone. He patted his old outboard. *If it starts first time, I'll try for the village,* he decided. Ruto gave the starter cord a heartless pull, but the still-warm pistons settled into a contented purr. Swearing softly he untied the skiff, leaned back and finished the bottle.

By the time he cleared the pass Ruto was drunk. He did not realize just how drunk until, a half mile from Fungamisi, he woke in darkness to a stalled engine and a strange voice screaming to be taken to shore. With shaking hands he switched fuel tanks and restarted the motor, its familiar drone a frail shield against terror. When the few lights of Fungamisi appeared to port, he rammed the beach at full speed, somersaulting over the bow into sand. The prop howled as he climbed to his feet, but the voice was even louder.

"Don't you dare run! Take me to land or I'll break your boat on a reef!"

Had it been his boat, Ruto would have fled anyway, but it was his father's and home-built. Dolefully, Ruto lifted the body out and staggered with it into the treeline. The thing was not so heavy without arms or legs, but he was sick from the whisky and scared, and the tapa was wet and stinking.

"Bury me in that pit! At the base of that broken trunk!"

The covered pit was hot as hell, but still Ruto rolled the body in. Once he had covered it back up with branches and banana leaves he ran as fast as he could to his cousin's house on the other side of the village. They drank kava until dawn, and when the sun had risen high enough went back in search of the pit. They could not find it, though.

SEMISI FALESI SAT in the third pew from the rear, admiring the orange glow of sunset through the church windows. The place seemed possessed by a vibrant holiness, an aura that warmed him from head to foot. *Thank you, Lord, for Your mercy and the gifts that You bring.*

The manna had come from nowhere. His wife thought a relation had left it, but a single taste affirmed the meat's true origin. There was nothing on earth so tender or sweet. Or so timely. Since the accident, their underground oven had smoked with pig and yam and fish, but after four days of feasting they were out of food with one mourning day left. Semisi had sent his boys over the island to borrow from relations, but supplies were scarce, and his sons lazy. There were times Semisi had thought of Toa as his only son. With Hunga Pass to his credit Toa would have become an important man in the kingdom. He could have secured Semisi the land title he wanted, and found some work for his brothers. But all this was gone, vanished in a puff of smoke and spray. After a sleepless night, Semisi had risen to face his final shame, only to find God's bounty awaiting, tapa-wrapped and perfectly cooked.

After much prayer Semisi bade his wife gather dalo leaves. They worked hurriedly, wrapping the sacred food into bundles, a single bite each. Their labour was not wasted; once the first few mourners arrived, word spread quickly. Everyone in the village visited Toa's shrine that day, as did those from Utelei and Paingo. All solemnly paid their respects before vying for their share of God's manna. By late afternoon Semisi estimated upward of one hundred people—including the Governor of Vava'u himself—had come. Even Toa's brothers roused themselves from sleep to partake. As evening approached Semisi set the last bundle atop

Toa's white-sand grave and thanked God for finding use for his son in heaven. But this was not the end of the story. No, he thought smiling, *this is only the beginning*.

Early that morning, he had awoken to the hammering of nails. Across the pitted road his neighbour Fafili was kneeling on hands and knees replacing a two-by-four that had long ago rotted on his weathered porch. Then Semisi smelled the smoke. He strolled down the pot-holed road to find neighbours gathering dead fronds and weeds from their yards. By late morning a dozen fires burned, and off the beach every mooring was vacant.

Shortly past noon the first of the fishing boats returned. From his porch Semisi heard the shouting and went to investigate. The launch was not big, but their catch was astounding. Huge grouper, rainbow runners, skipjack, even a yellow-fin tuna that must have weighed one hundred pounds at least. It was miraculous, the fishermen said. They had caught so many they had run out of bait. They were about to use guts when a male *mahi mahi* bit a bare hook trailing over the side! More boats returned, holds brimming, their tales echoes of joy. Scales shone like coins over the sand. Soon there were so many fish that selling them became pointless.

Walking home, Semisi saw an old pickup truck inching down the road. Its bed was full of gravel, and men with shovels followed, filling the foot-deep ruts. When he spotted his eldest son behind the wheel he rubbed his eyes, then looked again. Yes, there were the others, joking quietly together as they worked the gravel flat over each hole. Semisi dared not approach; he feared his presence might snap whatever spell had been cast over them. He turned and ran, taking a back route home to find his wife serving tea to the district head of the land department.

Pila looked like most Tongan officials: vast, overfed. When he smiled it was cannily, his cheeks so plump they squeezed his eyes into slits.

"Good morning, sir," said Semisi. "It's a pleasure to welcome you to our home."

"Thank you. Your wife said you would be home shortly."

Semisi perched uneasily on the edge of a chair, but Pila was in no hurry. He talked of the weather and the peculiar amount of work people were doing over in Utelei. He asked if the news of the great catch was true. Finally, after a third cup of tea he stood, thanked them for their hospitality and began to lumber toward his parked Land Rover. Halfway across the road, however, he stopped as though he had forgotten a favoured hat or his keys perhaps.

"By the way, the Governor paid me a visit last night. He says you may go ahead with your land project." He shrugged ruefully. "Who knows, maybe Toa spoke to him."

Now, sitting with his family in church, a wave of love surged through Semisi. If only Toa could have shared in this somehow. He followed the congregation forward for the sacrament, his eyes welling as the minister placed a wafer on his tongue.

"Take and eat of this."

THE WOMAN OF HIS CHOICE

THERE WERE SEVEN HUTS ON THE EAST SIDE OF THE river bend and Faero paddled his dugout through bora plants toward the largest one. A plume of smoke rose from each cooking fire and also from the small fire burning in a near-finished canoe. All inside the wall-less huts watched him and all knew why he had come and though he could not see Sumuina, her father rose from his hammock and walked down the *sisi* path toward the water. Idamo was short and thin with a hard pot-belly, his face carved with wrinkles around the eyes. He spoke no greeting, but stood and watched from above as Faero tied his dugout to a manglewood piling with twine. Halfway across the river Faero had removed his boots and placed them under the blanket spread before him. From under the same blanket he lifted out a handwoven cage and passed it up. Idamo took and turned the green koro parrot before his narrowed eyes and Faero waited for a smile, for any sign at all, but there was none so he steeled himself and spoke.

—*Aidatu*, we have important things to discuss.

Eyes still on the parrot, Idamo grunted.

—Yes, *neburatu*, I know why you have come, but there is time enough. First we will eat.

He turned and walked with the cage back toward the hut as Faero climbed from his canoe. Underfoot, the palmito shafts that formed the path were smooth and still warm from the day's spent heat.

Idamo's home was two huts joined together. As a canoe maker, he was rich from the labour of others and had fastened temiche blinds around one corner for sleeping but, like most Warao homes, the second hut had none. Past the old man's married daughters and sons-in-law in hammocks and his wife near the fire, Faero saw Sumuina appear from a path in the jungle. As he sat on the palmito floor he studied her quick steps, her fingers curling then relaxing as though uncertain which was proper. She was small, with thin calves, and wore a short dress like crepe paper tied at the neck and a mass of beaded necklaces that hid her throat entirely. She had not oiled her hair but Faero noticed a flush of *onoto* dye beneath her flat black bangs, and earrings with beads and shining Bolivar coins that swayed with each mannered step. As she entered the hut's square shadow she did not look at him, nor had she when Idamo first paddled her upriver to the resort with her dying child. Now she brought both men taro and *morocoto* fish and Faero felt the brush of her brown hand, slim like the rest of her but strong. Scenting the food, a village dog took a few shy steps toward him but she shooed it away then went and sat with her sisters and mother in the corner.

As Faero ate he felt the gaze of the other young men upon him. He timed his mouthfuls with Idamo's, but one son-in-law finished quickly and went on foot to fetch the village elders as his *arahi* instructed. Faero was no longer hungry but continued eating; he gazed out over the dark river with its floating bora rafts and reflected light spearing through the moriche and silka trees lining the far shore. He wished to break the silence but remained quiet and tossed his fish bones to the dogs when the old man did. Only then did the women begin to eat.

They were not long finished when Idamo's *dawa* reappeared on the path with what seemed like the whole small village in tow. As they filed under his roof Idamo's wife took the iron pot off the fire and placed fresh wood over the whitened coals. Greetings were murmured between relations as each one found a seat, then Idamo, who had not moved, began to speak.

—This is Faero's third visit to my hut, and I have asked that you gather here because you all have heard this *monikata*, and I want no more rumours.

He waved Sumuina near and once she was seated he took her hand and stroked the down of her arm and watched Faero closely.

—*Neburatu*, my daughter has told me you want her for your wife. Is this true?

—It is, *aidamo*.

—I have spoken with Sumuina and her mother is very glad, but I wish no deceptions. You know she has been already married?

—I do, *aidamo*.

—And that her husband was no good and I threw him from my home?

—Yes, *aidamo*.

—Do you know how to fish?

—I do, *aidamo*.

—Do you know how to clear fields?

—Yes, I do know.

—Do you know how to make canoes?

—Not so well as you, *aidamo*.

Those gathered laughed but the old man only nodded and pushed a burning brand farther into the fire.

—Much *monikata* surrounds you, *neburatu*, and this is why I have asked the elders here. We know you left the river and your good resort job and then returned. I have heard that you have since lost your job. Is this the truth?

—It is, *aidamo*.

—And I have been told that you lay with a white woman and it was for her you left your home. Is this also true?

When he nodded, Idamo lifted his gaze from the fire and regarded first Faero, then the assembled circle.

—You had a home and family and you threw them away. You had a good job with the resort people and you threw that away. You went with a white woman and you returned with nothing. *Neburatu*, our world is changing and I am old but I will not let you make a fool of me and my family. You can speak the Spanish and can work with *extranjeros*, but my daughter has suffered and I will not let her marry a boy too weak for manhood; we have enough mouths to feed.

A murmur rose around the fire Faero stared so deeply into. The sun had dropped and over the far shore the sky was rusting upward into night. Without looking at Sumuina, Faero rose, but Idamo caught his arm, his grip hard as polished bone.

—But as I said, I am an old man and Sumuina is no longer an *iboma*. She is not so young and should not be punished by my bad decisions. This one will be hers and the elders' alone. But first we must hear why you have returned and why you want her. If you are strong enough you will tell us the truth, and then the right decision will be clear.

In the darkening hut a ring of eyes reflected flame as Faero sank again to the floor. He had prepared for anything but this. Story was blood for Warao but his own made no sense to him, had no moral but shame. He arm pulsed where the old man had gripped his soot-filled scar and as silence gathered like cloud his sole urge was to flee. Instead, he turned his arm near the fire and read for them Gwethe's tattooed name.

HE HAD BEEN HALF A MILE from the resort when verandah lamps sprang from semi-darkness like a row of glow-flies. No one saw him slip between the supply and passenger boats and haul his dugout up the soft bank. He heard salsa from the long-house and an occasional burst of laughter as he threw his pack over one shoulder and strode toward the noise. The temiche roof looked traditional but was two stories high and electric lamps dangled from its thick manglewood beams. As he entered the side entrance he found the leather furniture dragged into a semi-circle, the couches and chairs filled by *extranjeros*. They were mostly women and young and there were more to his right at the small bar where Juanita stood pouring rum punches. Faero smiled his greeting to her and saw Angel near the front doors, but before he could approach, Chris—the tour operator—slipped inside the longhouse and called for people's attention. Chris was white and goateed and spoke in English. Everyone laughed as with a flourish he wheeled and threw wide the double doors. Faero had paddled five hours but fatigue dropped like his pack from his shoulders as Gwethe stepped from darkness into light.

She was blond and stout and wore a skirt of twine-stitched leaves that stopped high on her pale thighs. A bodice of the same design was stretched by heavy breasts and her curled hair was caught in a twist of purple bora blooms. A string of red pionias seeds was looped around her neck and some hung from her earlobes and more ringed one white ankle. A moriche train trailed along the floor and from behind her bare shoulders wide green banana leaves fanned like wings with each step. When she reached the semicircle she performed a slow pirouette as her audience whistled and clapped. Watching her retreat, Faero felt a pull like a current. Another in leaves made her entrance but he barely noticed her or the one that followed, or Angel, who stepped up behind him to speak. When the three women reappeared for judging, Faero fixed his gaze upon the first. Only when she noted his stare did he lift his pack and move with Angel toward the kitchen to eat.

The next morning he and Angel were up early, checking engines and fuel tanks and bailing last night's rain from the boats. Angel was from Ciudad Guayana and spoke perfect English. He had learned this was no ordinary group but Norwegian students who had been sent to Venezuela on a government program. They had spent three weeks at Chris's Playa Colorado camp and were to head downriver for another two. When Genado and Mocho appeared, the four of them shuttled supplies to an aluminum longboat, and once it was full Angel fired the engine and steered into the river and north. Students arrived with their bags and stood or sat on the verandah as above the koro parrots began their daily migration. Two wing-clipped macaws bobbed their blue heads and screeched as freer cousins flapped overhead.

When she came down the pathway she wore khaki shorts and a snug koro-green top. Faero owned few clothes but had chosen carefully that morning and his brown pants were tucked into rubber boots and his purple shirt front was open from collar to belly. Despite Angel's ribbing he also wore his leather-sheathed machete and his friend's straw vaquero hat. As she brought her bag to the dock-end, he beckoned and gripped its handle firmly so his forearm would bunch. When the last bag was loaded, he and Genado followed the students inside and ate eggs with black beans and coffee in the kitchen. He finished quickly then went with Juanita to the students' table to help clear. Taking the blonde's plate he was careful to drop nothing and approach from her right so she might see the anteater he had burned with a needle into his sheath. Then Chris appeared in the kitchen with a smile and sunglasses affixed and asked if the boat was ready. Faero said yes then asked what was the name of the girl in the blue shirt. Gwethe, Chris said, and smiled wider.

—*Cuidado, amigo. Las chicas Europeas son muy diferentes de las chicas de aquí.*

Chris led his group outside to be fitted with boots and Faero returned with Mocho to the boat. Ushering the group aboard, he was glad when Gwethe took the seat just aft of the wheel.

The sky was clear and the sun hot already as he pushed down the twin throttles. The heavy boat reared onto a plane and began skimming over the glass-skinned river and soon the resort vanished behind them. The wheel felt firm as Faero dodged rafts of bora plants and steered so close to shore they could brush manglewood with their hands. The engine's roar bounced off the close-passing leaves then disappeared as he made a spray-laden turn into a hidden *caños*. He grinned at the *extranjeros'* squeals, then nearly rammed a tree when Gwethe's bare foot brushed his thigh.

The second camp was sixty miles downriver. After the first hour the students fell silent as green shores unreeled on either side. On occasion they passed fishermen or family canoes piled high with supplies and Faero would slow their boat to prevent waves and then speed off again. He knew that to *extranjeros* the river seemed changeless but the closer they drew to ocean the darker the water turned as the jungle's rot steeped in it like tea. Ashore, the stands of moriche and temiche gave way to silka and sangrito as they entered another small channel with a bora-plant boom across its mouth. The passage was clogged with deadheads so they continued slowly, and around the next corner Faero reached and plucked off a water cocoa's bud and handed it to Chris. Holding the foot-long pod for all to see, Chris explained how this was his favourite Orinoco plant, then he reached out to Gwethe and asked her to blow on it. She blushed and shook her head but he smiled and said it would not hurt her. With a shrug she clasped the pod in both fists and dropped her mouth down its entire length.

Later Chris would explain that the mistake was his, not her clearly excellent English, but just then he was laughing too hard to speak. Gwethe's face flushed red but she still held the bud as her friends howled behind her. Once Faero recovered from his shock, he caught her hand and blew a warm stream of air over the plant. The thin pod parted in three, white- and scarlet-tipped hairs bursting forth like a blood-dipped brush. Behind them laughter morphed into amazement, and as the blossom passed aft, Gwethe leaned into him, whispered *Gracias*.

Above, the canopy kept the river dark as they rounded the final bend before camp. The roofs were temiche and so shrouded by jungle that no one noticed until they were almost dockside. Angel and Mocho appeared on the landing and tied their bow, then helped the passengers out. The dock joined a small verandah that was partially covered by roof and extended back from the water over a bar and picnic-tabled dining hall. A walkway led to the bare sleeping quarters and another toward the washrooms past an open kitchen and boat corral. Within the triangle of walkways lay a small herb garden and the steel legs of a water cistern shrouded by canopy thirty feet overhead. No generator ran, and for the first hour the students lounged on verandah chairs or walked the planked perimeter listening to the jungle sounds squeezing them in. Even at lunch they spoke quietly, as though afraid to disturb what lay sleeping mere feet from their newly slung hammocks. In the kitchen, the staff ate spaghetti with salad and orange juice from a mix. Chris approached and asked if they might go for a jungle walk. As Genado and Chris and Faero paddled canoes from the corral, Faero was glad to see Gwethe waiting on the landing. When she got into Genado's canoe, he felt his stomach clench.

There was little current so far from the main river. Genado led them upstream and chose a landing site, and once they had beached the canoes Faero was careful to keep his distance from her. The bank disappeared from sight in seconds and birds fell silent above the sound of breaking roots and squeals as the group stumbled deeper into the jungle. The sun remained high but hidden by canopy. Standing water sucked at their boots. Mosquitos died in blackwater, but the trees wore humid air like a cloak and each new stretch of jungle seemed indistinguishable from the old. As Chris described how the Warao survived here, Faero trimmed a five-foot temiche stem, then cut a broad leaf from a terite plant. With his fingers he stripped a pale three-foot filament from the back of the leaf and tied this to the end of his stem. Then from his pocket he drew a matchbook and tore and tied a small white paper corner to the filament's dangling tip. He trimmed another terite, then folded the broad leaf like cupped hands and fixed it with more thread, set it on his head, and stole toward a pool of standing water. When near enough he dropped into a crouch, flipped the bait into the pool, and twitched the paper on the surface. Students crept up around him and he feared they had frightened his prey until a small brown hoku fish darted from between rotting leaves. With a deft flick Faero flipped the fish up and caught it in the hat tipped down from his head like a creel. He turned, grinning, with his catch, but Gwethe was busy licking termites off Genado's hand. As others examined the fish Faero dropped his rod and walked, keeping an eye on the wide leaves around him. Moments later he froze, then beckoned Chris forward.

The spider was young and only as big as his fist. When he plucked it gently from a temiche leaf, its brown body was so light all he felt was the tingling trail of its anesthetic-tipped hairs. The group gathered as it walked his treadmilling hands. One boy extended his own hand and all was well until the spider crept past his biceps. Panicking, he flicked it and Gwethe's eyes grew wide when it landed on her, but she dared not move because the spider was angry, its half-inch fang poised near the swell of her nipple. Faero felt her pulse through his palm as he pressed against her and coaxed the spider onto his hand. After placing it high on a branch he walked without looking back to where Genado was hacking a palmito trunk with his knife. Soon the slim tree dropped and Faero cut free a three-foot section, split it lengthwise and drew the pale heart of palm out for the students to taste. As they ate, Chris took Genado's knife and shucked the outer husk, then with a splinter wrote JAKERA TOURS on the bark's inner flesh. He trimmed more sections for the others to try and Gwethe wrote, then passed her piece to Faero.

—*Mi nombre en Inglês.*

As he slipped the bark into his pocket, Faero saw how each plant and leaf possessed its own unique colour; with the light playing down through the canopy the jungle was beautiful in ways he had not seen before. So entranced was he by this new world that he soon lost all sense of direction. Wordlessly he let Genado forge ahead but, following, found him pissing against a tree. When he asked him which way to the boat the still-pissing Genado shrugged.

—I thought you knew.

The group looked hot and tired as Faero retraced their steps. *Extranjeros* rarely lasted long without the horizon; he and the other guides often laughed about this, but Faero did not feel like laughing now. He walked quickly and, faced with an expanse of standing water, was struck again how the jungle was like fish scales: one way smooth, the other rough and difficult. The growth seemed more dense and the water deeper, yet Faero dared not turn again because she would think him no hero but a fool. Sloshing through the pool he heard the *extranjeros'* own language and the fear in their foreign tones. Horseflies circled his head and his shirt clung like skin. His boots were full of water and behind him Gwethe's face looked flushed and anxious. When a shout rang out to his right Faero turned and caught a flash of reflected light; moments later he found Chris standing sheepishly beside the canoes. Faero beat his knife butt against a sangrito tree and, once Genado had answered with the same *boom boom boom*, he helped Gwethe into the smallest canoe and pushed off.

The sun was low and the air cool over the river. Gwethe sat with her back to him, trailing fingers through water, and when they reached the camp landing she walked off without a word. After tying up the canoes, Faero and Angel set the students' table for dinner, then went to the storeroom to get diesel for the lanterns. The lamps were soup cans with rope for wicks and as they walked the camp perimeter, Angel smiled up over yellow flame.

—That fat one's no Warao, *maraisa*. You better ask Chris before grabbing her big white *pechos*.

Faero scowled and told him the one person he'd ask permission was her father and her father was not here. And anyway she wasn't fat.

Grinning, Angel returned the fuel to the shed, then joined him in the kitchen, and after they'd eaten Faero walked out to the verandah with one of Angel's cigarettes. Despite the food and smoke, his insides felt hollow. When Gwethe stole up with her own cigarette and asked for a light he passed her his and she touched and held the ends together until the ember subdivided. Above them, the sky was orange but fading as koro parrots and macaws winged home from the feeding grounds. He pointed up and in slow Spanish explained that their other name was *aves d'amor* because each pair mated for life. Her laughter felt like hooks in his skin and he rose angrily but she touched his arm and pointed to where a dark line of cloud reefed the horizon.

—*Algunas noches en Noruega las montañas se veían así.*

He asked her what a mountain was, and she said a stone hill so big you had to look skyward to see its top. The day's sun had brought out freckles on her nose and shoulders but under her upturned chin the skin looked soft, paper-white. Above her, one star shone through and Faero pointed and said the first Warao had lived there. Once a hunter shot but missed a deer with his bow, and when he pulled the arrow from the ground he found a world full of moriche and fish and game. People began to jump through the hole until a pregnant woman tried and got stuck. Men pushed from above and men pulled from below but she stayed stuck and that star was her shining anus. He told her the Warao believed that they were in heaven already and when they died they would have to return to that harder star world. When she asked if he was in paradise he gazed at her and said not yet.

Chris strolled from the dining room and sat between them. Soon other students followed and began to ask Faero questions about delta life. With Chris translating, he talked about building canoes from cachicamo logs bent open by long-fires and learning Spanish at the mission and harvesting crops for the fathers as a child. He told them about Sister Micaola, who liked singing, and Sister Innocencia, who had died. When they asked him about Warao women, he spoke of gathering wood and sago starch and weaving hammocks and giving birth in canoes—and now they knew why Warao meant "people of the canoe." He explained how when a boy wanted a girl he would cleave a piece of wood with one machete stroke to prove his worth. When Gwethe asked if he had ever done this, he blushed but said nothing. Above them, the sky was cobalt and star-pocked, and as students trickled back to their hammocks Gwethe talked about Norway. She told him about winding channels cut into the land and four-hour days and cathedrals and cold and no parrots but for those in cages. She spoke of school and a boy she did not miss and how far away it all seemed, how small. She asked if he had been to a city and he said no. She asked if they might take a canoe out on the river.

There was no wind and the water was smoked glass that their canoe creased soundlessly but for the drips off his paddle. Two hundred feet past the landing a small roof ghosted into sight. She leaned back against his legs and he stroked her hair, then she turned and tilted her face up to him. Her lips were soft and plump and her tongue slid into his mouth tasting of nicotine and mint and though his teeth clicked against hers she pressed harder. Fingertips traced his thighs then slipped between them, kneading him stiff while his own hands wandered. He reached lower and found her slick and warm but her mouth warmer as he leaned back, the sky tilting in a slow cartwheel. Then she was above him blocking the stars. Hair showered his face, the smell of her, her breasts warm sacks, the weight of a world pressing down.

SHE HAD BEEN GONE TEN DAYS when Chris arrived with his next group. Faero waited on the landing and she was not there and soon enough those who were grew invisible. He carried their bags and did chores and taught them how to catch piranha and tarpon and made them terite-leaf hats, but their delight meant nothing to him. Even the boat-driving he loved so much grew joyless because each turn taken came to the same end: the river he had always known and would never leave. He asked Chris how Gwethe was and he said fine, she was working with a local school near Playa Colorado. At the lower camp Faero took a canoe out and drifted past the owner's unlit hut.

On their second night together she had steered them ashore, lit a foil-wrapped candle and led him inside. The hut was small with only a net-draped mattress at its centre. She parted the mesh and he followed and by candlelight she undressed and showed him things impossible in hammocks. When he could go no more she lifted the candle and its hot drips brought him back; moving within her he had never felt so needed or strong. Later, his head on her breasts, she spoke more of Norway and what he would learn when he returned with her. She told him about castles and cafés and how much people would pay for the baskets he wove, but most importantly how they would be together in their own big bed. As she spoke, the candlelight played on the mosquito net and behind it the jungle disappeared. They returned to the hut every night after that, and as she talked Faero began to see old streets and mountains on the billowing walls until the mesh brushed flame and burned a three-foot hole.

The day they arrived back at the first camp Faero was too miserable to take out a canoe. Instead they sat together on the dock, smoking in silence, and as the blue night shrank from dawn Faero realized time was no ally. After breakfast Gwethe kissed his cheek at the landing and told him to write, then she stepped aboard, waving as Angel brought the boat up onto a plane and vanished around the bend. As though she had never been. Later Faero collected his pay and paddled home and nothing had changed but that the hammock his mother was weaving was a foot wider. She accepted a ten-pound bag of rice and he gave his father cigarettes and they smoked and talked about the still-broken motor as his sisters prepared their meal. When Faero asked him what a city was like his father thought for a moment, then said: Loud.

After they'd had their fill of rice and sago bread his sisters and brothers-in-law stayed near the fire but Faero went and lay in his hammock. He watched a pale moon rise over the trees and tried to sleep and not think about Gwethe. Her scent still on his hands, he imagined her in them, flesh soft between fingers gliding over the swell of her stomach. He imagined the feel of it stretched by his growing child, taunt as a water-skin, milk-white. Later in the dark he heard a couple making love, and compared to his own memories their sounds were like rooting pigs at the mission. When they were finished and sleeping Faero rose from his hammock, blew into the fire's dim coals and took from his bag the piece of palmito Gwethe had given him. Setting a blackened pan over flame he straightened out one of his fish hooks, and once old grease was hissing hot he scraped the tip inside then pushed it through the skin of his arm. The welling blood looked black and the pain was real but strangely soothing as he returned the hook to the pan. Once he had traced her name he took ash and rubbed it into his wounds and only then did he remount his hammock and sleep. The next morning he rose early to fish and caught between paddling upstream or down knew it made no difference. The next time Chris prepared to leave the delta, Faero said he would go with him.

The day was hot like every other and the clouds were building into storms over sea as Chris took off his sunglasses and faced him.

—*El mundo es muy diferente fuera del río. Gwethe es muy diferente tambiên. ¿Tû sabes?*

He prepared to say more, then put his sunglasses back on instead.

Faero was in the boat loading baggage when the canoe appeared downriver. He straightened and regarded the man paddling and the young girl hunched over her bundle in the dugout's bow. She was bent so low she looked broken and did not glance up when her canoe bumped the side of the speedboat. The old man grasped their gunwale to steady himself.

—Greetings, *maraisa*, are you well?

—I am, and you, *aidamo?*

—Well enough for an old man but my granddaughter is sick. No doctor has come to the river clinic for many weeks.

Faero's gaze drifted from man to girl. Black hair covered most of her face but she looked perhaps fifteen. When her infant coughed the sound was as wet and feeble as a drowning pup. Faero had heard the same sound when his own nephew had died. He looked back at the old man and saw little hope there.

—You go upriver now, *maraisa?*

—Yes, but the boat is full.

—There will be another boat?

—Yes, but only tomorrow.

Behind them, *extranjeros* began to file out to the landing, their gazes set as though to fix the scene in place. One drew out a camera and had others pose beneath the resort sign. When she turned and saw father and girl in the dugout she aimed and snapped another picture. The old man watched Angel help them into the speedboat, then turned back to Faero.

—*Maraisa*, are you also heading upriver?

Faero nodded.

—Then you can wait until tomorrow.

—No, *aidamo*.

—And why not?

Before he could answer, Chris stepped from the longhouse.

—*¿Cuántos días estuvo enferma?*

—*Trieze, quatro días*, said her father.

—*¿Eres tú el padre?*

Shadow passed over the old man's face.

Chris shook his head and told Faero to make room.

At her father's command the girl's head rose and her face was plain and terrified. Chris jumped onto the flat bow to help her aboard. When she passed him the child she did this so anxiously it was as though even brief separation might snap the sole thread keeping it alive. Once the last student had squeezed in, Angel fired the engines and the old man pushed off with his paddle and watched them climb onto a plane until there was nothing left but the spreading V of their wake. Wind curled around the bow and whipped the girl's black hair. Chris spread his coat over her bare legs but she did not notice. So intently did she cradle her child that she remained motionless for the whole two-hour trip. Carving round the last bend before town, Faero wished to ask how with all she had seen could she expect something as unlikely as a cure, but he did not.

At the dock they unloaded and he led her past mango trees and up the sun-baked street. He asked a passing *criollo* if the doctor was in but he only shrugged. Gripping the girl's arm he marched her toward the clinic's blue cross and locked door and peered through the dust-smudged glass. Another *criollo* stood in a shadowed archway. Asked when the doctor would come, the man said maybe today, maybe never, though God knew he was still getting paid by the *gobierno*. There was no breeze between the buildings, and as the girl wiped her child's slack mouth Faero heard the Land Cruiser start up. Swiftly he led her back to the dock. Across the brown river, trees looked far away and foreign as he told Angel to take her home, that nothing more could be done. Released, she stood like a game piece on a board and Faero wished to be anywhere but near this river, these Warao, their endless toil and drudgery and the violent growth of jungle.

Angel removed his vaquero hat and set it gently on Faero's head.

—*Para la suerte, amigo.*

In the packed Cruiser, students hunched along both sides on benches. What luggage had not fit on the roof lay under their knotted legs. Faero climbed into the seat beside Chris and fixed his eyes on the broken road.

—*¿Qué pasa con el médico?*

—*Él no está aquí.*

—*Prodríamos llevarla el doctor en Temblador.*

—No, viene hoy más tarde; es mejor si ella espera aquí.

Chris studied him through mirrored sunglasses, then turned and slipped the truck into gear.

The world changed swiftly away from the river. They had not gone half a mile before trees gave way to savannah dotted by squat barns and ranches and shallow mud ponds. The track was pitted gravel with a poled power line running alongside. Turning onto a paved crossroad, Chris accelerated until the flat yellow landscape was flying past the windows. To Faero it felt a bit like boating. He watched cars in the opposite lane, loving how he had to pan his head slowly, then quickly, as they passed. On the horizon a dark line drew nearer and he saw it was jungle, but unlike any jungle he had ever seen. The trees were straight and needled and so green they looked black. For half an hour their ruled rows flickered sunlight, hemming them until they passed another junction and savannah again took over.

Temblador was the largest town Faero had seen. Bright-signed stores flaunted clothing in windows and music blared from loudspeakers, but there were no Warao anywhere. Beside a drink-stand, a *criollo* with one foot hobbled on crutches made of wood blocks nailed together. The blocks were perfectly machined but so ill-suited for their task that Faero could only stare. As the man limped past, the students piled back into the truck, and soon they had left the town behind. Beer was handed out and there was much laughter as they sped north. Refinery stacks flamed like candles and thick pipelines reared from the ground and paced their grey river of road. When they crested a long rise, land unrolled below them and Faero had not known earth could be wider than sky. Chris dialled his cellphone and warned his wife they were two hours away. Ada was Colombian and dark-eyed and eight months pregnant. After he hung up, Faero asked if he was excited about fatherhood. When Chris nodded yes, Faero smiled and said so was he.

Green gave way to yellow to scrub forests that faded as the soil dried nearer the coast. Trucks kicked up dust contrails. Tall buildings began to rise in the distance and there was more traffic as their road wound through scrub-covered hills. The hilltops were high above, and Faero asked if these were mountains but Chris shook his head.

The ground near Puerto la Cruz looked razed. Crowds of tin-roofed huts kneeled in muddy yards among garbage and children and gutted cars. The sky smoked. Skirting the city limits, they passed rows of oil-storage tanks by the road, which neared then followed the edge of the sea. Faero peered over cliffs where rust-brown islands sank offshore like limestone ramps. Impossibly large ships swung at anchor near a huge ash-coloured complex cut into the side of a hill. When he looked again the islands had turned green and the forest had thickened as they curved down the spine of another ridge. The beach at its foot was not white but smooth and sun-bright the way Gwethe described snow. Rather than turn toward it Chris steered them up a steep road and parked outside a high-bricked wall. He opened the chain-link fence and Faero followed him inside.

The courtyard was green with cut grass shaded by old mango trees. A ginger dog loped soundlessly toward them and only when Faero reached to pet him did he see the cappuccino monkey riding its coat like a four-fisted cowboy. Following the cement walk to the house he saw a flash of blond in one doorway and his chest clenched. The bungalow was L-shaped with a tin roof overhanging the inside corner where several Warao-made hammocks were slung. From the door of the kitchen Ada stepped out, dark-haired and huge, but when she saw Faero her eyebrows rose. Chris spoke rapidly in English and Ada turned to Faero, her smile fixed as she told him to follow. They walked back to the road past the deserted truck and down through the gate of another house, this one square but with the same covered patio with hammocks in rows. The unloaded bags lay outside in a pile and there was much Norwegian and laughter from within until Ada called Gwethe's name.

The light was low and slanted between trees as she appeared in the doorway. She wore a fish-print sarong and the same parrot-blue top he loved, but when she saw him standing in his purple shirt and boots and straw vaquero hat she choked back laughter, then fled into the house. Stalking after her, Ada told Faero to stay where he was, but there was no danger of his moving: his feet were rooted to the ground. In the eternity that followed several girls took turns strolling out and staring, then Ada reappeared and shook her head. Faero surged for the door but she caught his arm.

—*No, hombre. Por favor.*

He asked her what about the baby.

—*¿Que nino?* she said, hand on her belly. *Mios?*

—*No. Mios.*

She shook her head again. His skin burned as Ada led him from the courtyard. Underfoot the road was a hard dead thing and never had he longed so much for river.

ONLY A FIST OF COALS GLOWED in the clay hearth. Idamo's wife rose and fetched wood, and when she had laid it over the fire Faero finished his story. How for days he haunted Chris's home and did not leave except to walk the beach and once to visit the tour office in Puerto La Cruz. He told them of tall buildings and traffic and restaurants and stores with lights like coloured constellations and how the ocean was too dirty to rinse the shore. He spoke of street vendors and goods too expensive to buy and the Warao and Pemon Indians he'd seen at the roadside waving money jars at passing cars. The heat and stink of the place snuffed dreams of snow-covered streets, but when he returned to the delta it seemed different, drained of colour. Then the resort owners arrived, found the burned mosquito netting and fired him. That same week he drank every Bolivar he'd saved to build his own camp and though drunk and fighting all comers it was not Gwethe's face that haunted him but a Warao girl's with her dying child. Angel told him where to find her, and though Idamo had threatened him he had come back and would keep coming until Sumuina took him as her man. He was done with drinking and would find a new job because more camps were being built even now. Soon she would have a hut and money and children to replace what she had lost.

Then he fell silent, but no sound rose from the close circle. He looked up from the fire and some met his gaze, but not Sumuina, and he knew his words had sunk him.

—Her name was Zanuca.

Sumuina's voice was leaden but still she pulled a brand from the fire and passed it to the nearest elder. The old man measured its strength and girth, gazed at her, then passed it on. The brand went from elder to elder until at last it reached Idamo. He did not look at the wood in his hand, only at his daughter beside him, and then he rose and held one end out to her. Despite its coals she grasped the brand firmly and Faero stood and in one smooth arc of his knife cleaved it in two. A shout went up, and those gathered stood and nodded to Idamo then made their way from the hut. Suddenly alone with his new family, Faero felt he should say something but the thought exhausted him. Instead he led Sumuina to the water, helped her into his dugout and pushed them from shore.

The pre-dawn blue paled to white as he paddled, and when they reached the river's heart he let current take hold. Sumuina turned but looked through him. Since finding her, Faero had moved with the will of one carving a canoe. Now wavelets lapped against wood and the river kept them up. Always these same elements: sky and wood and water. How he could lose something unseen or owned baffled him, but it was so. As low cloud scarred the horizon he studied Sumuina's soft face: she might not know how clouds resembled mountains, but loss she understood. When her eyes met his, he reached for her.

Snaring both hands, she gently pushed them back.

DROWNING IN AIR

TUELEN BECAME A CARVER WHEN HE WAS SEVENTEEN years old. One morning he was fishing alone in his father's skiff when a soft yet stern voice he had never heard before told him to turn and look toward his island. Inside its reef, the lush bulk of Pohnpei stretched across the horizon, brooding beneath a thick blanket of cloud. Tuelen was about to turn back to his fishing line when three dolphins broke water right in front of him, then vanished with barely a ripple. He waited, but they never resurfaced.

When Tuelen returned home, his family's shack was empty. The workshop was also deserted, his father's carving bench bare but for a rough piece of mangrove wood and an adze. He bent and picked up the wood, traced its grain with thin fingers. Then he sat and hefted the adze, admiring its balance, the feel of the smooth handle. Tuelen did not rise from the bench until the dolphins were again before him, their forms alive in his hands.

His father, Villi, told the story to all who would listen. How he had found the boy in his workshop covered in chips, the adze biting so swiftly and surely the wood seemed to melt into form.

His son's eyes were barely open; if he could hear, he gave no sign. When Tuelen's brothers and mother returned from the town market, they ate with Villi in silence, listening to the soft scrape of the chisel through the screen door. Re-entering the workshop, Villi discovered the tool had grown dull in his son's hand, but rather than stop the boy, he went next door and borrowed another from a cousin. Tuelen's hand was like a claw; Villi had to pry his fingers free to exchange tools. He sat with Tuelen for another three hours, sharpening, changing the blades twice more. These were the only times his son looked at him. Once, as an experiment, Villi stood and switched off the bare bulb that hung from the rafter. The chisel's scrape carried on unhindered. When the carving was complete Tuelen did not stop to admire it. He just set it down, leaned back on the bench and fell asleep.

By mid-morning the next day the whole village had seen Tuelen's work. Dolphins were a popular subject for the Kapingamarangi carvers, but not like these. The trio were not mounted with dowel on a base but rather grew from wave-shaped swirls like the ocean spirits they were. They seemed alive, wonderful and strange. That they had been carved by a boy who had never held an adze before was stranger still.

"Perhaps he has been practising in the boat," one brother suggested.

"Father must have been teaching him in secret," said Goro, the eldest, envy bright in his eyes. But they and everyone else knew no such thing could be true. In a village famed for woodwork, Tuelen was the one boy who had refused to have anything to do with it. Even as a child the toys Villi carved did not fascinate, and when the boy grew older the tools, the wood and the money they earned held no interest for him. Tuelen chose the sea instead. By age fourteen he was a fine spear-fisherman. He could hold his breath longer and dive deeper than men twice his age and experience. Still, the family needed money and his father resented the boy's scorn for his trade.

"It is time for you to stop fooling around; you never catch many fish with your spear. If you want to be a part of this family, you have to help this family! Either fish outside the reef with a line or learn to carve like your brothers."

Tuelen took one look at the quaint flying fishes and carved sharks littering the workshop and chose fishing.

But his dolphins changed all that. The next morning neither his father nor his carving was to be found, so Tuelen hefted the gas tank and some bananas and marched the winding path down to the skiff. It was a typical day, hot and sunny out away from land. He caught three rainbow runners in the first hour. Then, with a glance toward Pohnpei, Tuelen checked his position with lineups using familiar points on land. Yes, he would drift over it shortly. He tied the fishing line off on a small cleat, dug his snorkel and mask out from under the seat and peered through his glass window into the blue.

Beyond Pohnpei's main reef, a coral mount rose from the depths like the head of some drowned forgotten giant, its crest fifteen feet down. Tuelen took a deep breath and plunged under, kicking deeper until the reef's gnarled bulk filled his vision. A young grouper ghosted from its den, saw him and disappeared. Bright parrotfish winged through the water, white trails of excrement like jet streams behind them. A school of stripers, electric-blue and yellow, twitched in unison over the coral head, then split as though cut by a knife. The blue-silver trevally was young, only a foot and a half long from the scowl of its blunt face to the sharp tips of its tail. With his last few seconds of air, Tuelen admired the grace of its design—the swept-back dorsal and anal fins, the slim power of its knobbed tail stalk—then he kicked upward.

He broke surface fifty feet from the skiff, and as he neared, Tuelen saw his fishing line twitching to and fro. He kicked hard and hauled himself into the boat, quickly untying the bucking line. He was lucky: had the fish been bigger it would have already broken free. Tuelen paid off some of his line's loose coils. On the other end the fish relaxed; its thrashing turned to widening circles. When Tuelen began drawing on the line, he did this so gently that his prey felt only the same, strength-sapping pull. Like the swing of a pendulum, its circles grew smaller and faster as it neared the surface, but when the fish saw the boat it bolted. Tuelen was ready; the wet coils he had prepared whipped off easily, and his fingers maintained just enough tension to ensure that the hook remained in place. He had to use this ploy twice more before he could draw the trevally close enough. On the next pass, Tuelen stood suddenly and drove his spear through the fish.

Once aboard, the trevally banged against the bottom of the boat, its lidless eyes staring everywhere at once. Tuelen coiled his line and watched the final twitches as death approached. It was not the same fish he had seen swimming, but still, a wave of regret washed over him. It seemed dishonest that a man could catch fish without even seeing the world he so artlessly tossed lures into. To spear you had to respect the fish; you had to become the fish to even get near it. He lifted the trevally gently off the floor and rinsed its still body in the waves. The lifeless form reminded Tuelen of the carvings his father sold to tourists: the right shapes and proportion, but empty, shadows of what they sought to represent.

Not until the skiff was carving back through the swell toward Pohnpei did Tuelen consider the night before. It was the strangest thing; he remembered sitting at the bench, then his father appeared as if from a dream to press a new chisel into his hand. Then he woke. Tuelen tried to recall the dolphins he had seen, their flowing movement, the way they lifted from water, and could not. He raced up the steep path to the village, anxious to see the carving. As he passed between shacks, the people who saw him whispered and grinned behind their hands. Tuelen grew worried by their odd behaviour. What had they heard? *Perhaps Father is angry that I used his wood,* he thought. *Perhaps he is going to throw me out on the street!* He quickened his pace and slipped through the door of their shack.

His mother stood by the basin working dough for their dinner bread in a cotton dress more grey than white. She turned to him without expression.

"Your father is waiting in the workshop."

Heart skipping in his chest, he laid the day's catch down and stepped slowly out the back door. His father stood with Tuelen's brothers, talking sternly, the dolphin trio cradled in one hand. Even from a distance, Tuelen was mystified. He was about to step forward to examine it when something else caught his eye. Under the warped corrugated roof now stood two benches, his father's and another one newly constructed. He saw his brothers' jealous anger, the pride in his father's face, and a great weight settled on Tuelen's shoulders. Beaming, Villi held out an adze blade.

"You must make the handle yourself. Only the carver knows what best suits his hand. I will show you how tomorrow." Villi stared down at the dolphins balanced on his other palm, then passed them to Tuelen. "I have never seen anything like them." His voice caught in his throat, and he hurried through the door into the shack.

As his brothers stormed off toward the apprentice shed, Tuelen traced the carved waves with his fingertips. He wanted to explain to his father what had happened, but how? He did not understand himself. There they lay in his hand, a smooth and perfect mystery.

The next day Tuelen did not go fishing. Instead, he sat with his father in the workshop, fashioning a handle for his adze.

"It will take time to find the perfect fit," Villi explained. "As your wrist grows strong the balance will change." He showed Tuelen how to fasten the handle with whipping cord over and under the blade.

Tuelen studied his father beside him. Villi's black hair was thick and wiry, his nose spread flat over a narrow face. He was tall but slouched horribly, and his brown eyes were always cast downward. This was the closest he had been to the man in a very long time, and though the adze felt awkward and strange, Tuelen grinned and bent to his task.

That evening, a taxi arrived at the village. The tourists that emerged were faceless above their crisp, First World clothing. Their guidebooks had described the carvers of Kapingamarangi; they wished to see these wares for themselves. Strolling from shack to shack, they studied the men's carvings and the woven pandanus of the women. There was much merchandise available: dolphins, flying fish, mantas and sharks with real baby shark's teeth. Tuelen watched them peruse his father's work. They wished souvenirs: passionless figures for obligatory gifts. Some were purchased, it did not matter which. Like supermarket tins they were easily replaced. Money changed hands. The tourists retreated toward the road.

Villi was about to close his display doors when, from behind them, a curt voice spoke up:

"Leave it, please."

Tuelen turned to see a small white woman with grey hair and glasses step into the light of the workshop's hanging bulb. She wore a shirt of loose cotton khaki pants, sandals and no jewelry but a chain so silver it looked white. Another taxi had brought her; the driver lurked a few steps behind. Villi drew back from his display, watched her quietly. Behind thick lenses, her eyes moved over the carvings, taking their measure in moments.

"They're very nice, but not what I'm looking for. Cheers." She turned to leave.

Villi touched her arm gently.

"Wait, Miss. Please, we have something else."

He vanished into the shack, reappearing moments later with the dolphin trio in his hands. When her small fingers cupped it Tuelen knew it was gone. He turned and fled the light of the workshop's naked bulb, looking for somewhere to hide. He tripped over the trunk of a fallen palm, then sat down. He hated the woman, but he hated his father more for offering up his carving so easily. How could he do this to him?

When Tuelen finally returned to the shack, music from the family's transistor radio struggled against uproarious laughter. He peeked in the door to find his father leaning back in a chair beside a case of Budweiser, Tuelen's uncles sitting with his brothers on the floor. When Villi saw him he jumped up and gave Tuelen a bear hug, laughing continuously.

"One hundred dollars, Tuelen! For your very first carving! Can you believe it? God is watching over us! Think of how rich we will be!" He turned and faced the revellers. "The future of the Timalu family! Goro, give him a beer!"

That night and for many days after, Tuelen tried to please his father. He toiled long hours for three weeks, completing several carvings. He refused to show them to anyone, however. Tuelen knew they were as soulless as everyone else's, and, even worse, their proportions were wrong. Soon Villi grew cross with him, and when the money from the sale dwindled, crosser still.

"What, are you playing with me, boy? Look, you're not even holding the adze right! I'm surprised you can carve your name in a tree with control like that!"

Tuelen bent his head. He could not argue: the one proof of his talent was gone.

The next morning, Tuelen rose earlier than usual. He dug his spear and fishing line out from under his tools in the workshop, hefted the gas tank and made for the beach. Once the outboard was running he steered out of the harbour, snaking between coral heads past the hulk of Sokehs Rock. Beyond land's protection, the sea breeze blew the last shavings from his hair. He headed for the sunken reef, grinning.

Sun stirred the deep with golden shafts as he dove and kicked his way down. It was like coming home. Stripers flowed around him like a rock-split river. He smiled to their silent music, waved at the young grouper half hidden in its lair and turned to see two great Napoleon wrasses cruising in tandem before he was forced to resurface. The skiff was still close and he dove again, loving the weighted embrace of depth on lungs and skin. *I should live here,* he thought to himself. Here was life, not dead shapes in dead wood. The two wrasses paced him curiously. Both adults, they were at least one hundred pounds each, their prominent snouts pushing out from under the large bump of their foreheads. He wanted to touch them, but they were far too timid and his breath too short for that. He would not fish that day, Tuelen decided at the surface. He would just swim. He duck-dove and sank deeper, the sea holding him close.

On the northern edge of the reef was a coral section outgrown from the rest. Two long fingers of trumpet coral reached out, and a huge sea fan waved placidly between them. It looked like a door, and the fish that emerged was big, bigger than any Tuelen had ever seen. Shaped like a massive grouper but jet black, it wore armoured scales as dark as the pupil in its monstrous eye.

Tuelen kicked himself alongside. *You are huge,* Tuelen thought admiringly.

But not always, replied the fish. *The last time you saw me I was three dolphins.*

Comprehension ran through Tuelen in a shiver. Together, they swam deeper than he had ever dreamed. Fish of every description emerged from the reef's protection, circling thickly around them until they formed one shimmering globe of colour. It was the most beautiful thing Tuelen had ever seen, but beside his joy was a tremendous sadness. Such a sight could never be reproduced, no matter how practised or skilled the hand. *If I could save even a fragment of this*, he thought. Tuelen turned back to the fish drifting beside him: serene, all-powerful.

I want to carve again.

The huge eye seemed to narrow as it swivelled to take Tuelen in.

Then breathe.

Tuelen broke the surface like a sleeper from dreams. After the sombre darkness below, the sun was blinding, and without the weight of water pushing him down he felt light, light enough to fly. The skiff had drifted a long way. He swam hard for many minutes before catching it.

TUELEN TOLD NO ONE what he had seen. It had been too beautiful, too unsettling. In the weeks that followed he did not know what he would be the next day, carver-apprentice or fisherman. When at sea he returned frequently to the sunken reef but he never again saw the great fish. This did not really surprise him, but he kept visiting anyway. In the workshop, he and his father worked without speaking, the old man chipping away at tired shapes, while Tuelen willed his hands to learn. And his technique improved; there was no doubt. Skill grew with each callus, but this brought Villi little joy. The works his son fashioned were strange, curious twists and knobs of wood. Even the few recognizable forms were worthless in his eyes.

"Why did you have to do that, boy? That fin was fine the way it was and now you've ruined it trying to get to that grain! Look how fragile it is! No one is going to buy something so delicate;

they'll never get it home in one piece! Can't you just let it alone for once? You can't sell a shark with a broken fin!"

His son studied the wood impassively, and Villi swore. There seemed no getting through to the boy; it was as though he was listening to another voice that blotted out anything he said. Villi threw up his hands and stormed from the workshop. Tuelen took no notice. All he could think was that if he had reached that grain it would have been perfect. Not a perfect shark, no, but the fin itself would have been a fragment of beauty, carving air the way the real ones carved water.

For the rest of the night, Villi would not speak to him, nor would his brothers. Tuelen studied their anger in silence. He had tired of explaining what he was reaching for; he preferred to suffer abuse and continue working. Despite his mother's passive support, his became an increasingly lonely existence at home, and the sea offered little respite.

After a month of diving nowhere but his reef, Tuelen began combing other stretches in the miles of water around Kolonia Harbour. He saw many amazing fish. Swimming out of a small cave cut into the coral, he surprised a school of twelve eagle rays winging silently along the wall. He saw grouper, octopus, white and black tips as well as many reef sharks; once, even a young whale shark. As the gap-mouthed monstrosity cruised from the depths toward him Tuelen was certain this was his fish, its new form chosen. But no voice spoke to him, and no image planted itself in Tuelen's mind. Finally, he returned to the lone reef, its coral faces as familiar now as his own. Kicking down past the jutting pinnacles and waving sea fans, he turned and swam with the current for a time, then worked his way toward the glimmering surface. A school of mackerel danced in the sun around his skiff. He pulled himself out and watched them a while. *Why won't you show yourself?*

Years ago, Villi had carved a bow and arrow for his sons. Tuelen and the others had played with them for hours until a village pig was foolishly shot and the bow broken over their backsides. He still remembered the sound of arrows, the whiff of feathers on the shaft as they disappeared into the distance. That is how the kestrel sounded as it streaked mere inches overhead. The bird struck the water and school simultaneously, resurfacing with a stunned fish crosswise in its dagger-like bill. For a moment the kestrel paused, wings outstretched, poised for flight. One yellow eye fixed on Tuelen, then the bird flapped itself free and was gone. Tuelen turned and started the outboard, gunning the skiff back home as fast as it would carry him.

It was not like the first time. His hands worked and he watched, as fascinated as Villi—faithful servant once more—to see the wood melt into form. But as the bird materialized before them, Tuelen felt a burning in the back of his throat. Yes, these were his hands, enlivened once more, and there was his father beside him, rejuvenated by pride. Beauty was clawing free before his very eyes, but what meaning did it have? The bird would be finished, and for all this blessed dexterity his hands would return to their earthly stupidity. Before the carving was complete, Tuelen already wondered to whom it would be sold and for how much. He suspected his father was thinking the same. Tuelen's hands worked the chisel around the small, stunned fish now clamped forever in the kestrel's sharp beak. *I am that fish,* he thought. *My one gift descends like death, leaves me nothing but longing.*

WINTER WAS HARD ON TUELEN. The few degrees' drop in temperature was enough to make his nights cold because his soul was cold already. Months had passed since he had finished the bird. The carving lasted a week before being sold, this time for $150. He had not been around for the sale. He returned one night from fishing and his bird was gone. As he'd expected, its completion had not made things easier. If anything, things got worse. The kestrel proved his dolphins were no fluke, and increased the pressure to produce again. Tuelen tried to ignore this and continued working, and his own skill improved until he was level with most of the village men. But his momentary brilliance now worked against him. Now nothing he produced on his own would satisfy them. Impossibly, he found himself more isolated than before. He lasted another month in the workshop before his father lost his temper and threw him out. Tuelen found the forest a quiet enough place to work in, but at night, curled on his beaten mattress as the dark breathed around him, his body ached, empty, inconsolable.

"What is it you want of me?" he cried one day as he floated listlessly in the skiff. "The villagers laugh when I pass. My brothers say my tools are cursed and won't go near them, and I only get leavings from wood no one else wants."

Who do you wish to honour, boy?

Tuelen looked quickly around. There was nothing but terns working a school of mackerel a hundred yards away.

"Only you," he whispered and leaned over the gunnel, ready for anything.

The boat gave a violent lurch. Tuelen found himself in the water, coughing violently, the salt burning his eyes and throat. He stole a ragged breath as, from nowhere, a steep wave broke over his head. The sea seemed to drag him under. His clothes weighed heavily on him, restricting his limbs as he fought, and for the first time in memory Tuelen was afraid of water.

Look.

Tuelen cracked open his eyes, then blinked and opened them wider. His vision was perfect. He could see farther than he ever had before and there was no sting from the salt. He pawed his face to check if somehow through some trick his snorkel mask was on, but there was only the rubbery texture of skin. He peered into the darkness of deep ocean, fear abandoned through the wonder of sight. *It is a shame I'm not over the reef,* he thought. *The things I would see.*

Look harder.

At first there was just awareness, a sense of motion where before there was nothing. Then a growth of darkness from lighter darkness, the shift of shadow to shape out of infinite depth. The manta approached like heaven and hell combined, demonic, had it not been for the undulations of wings. Tuelen watched in awe as its blue-black back passed inches beneath him, whiptail trailing like a broken tether. Then it curved away, turned and continued its loop inverted. The ray's mouth gaped wide, its white belly blue-speckled and smooth but for two flushing gills.

I love you. Tuelen reached out one hand.

So you say. The tip of one wing curled, sending the ray into a slow twisting spiral.

You do not believe me?

The huge form turned and passed by him so closely that he found himself staring into the ray's small black eye.

I will always believe in you; that is my curse. You will never wholly believe; that is yours.

The manta winged away, fading into the blue, so full and empty. Tuelen stared after it for some time before again feeling the salt sting, his lungs burning for air. The skiff had drifted so far he had to strip off pants and shirt to swim fast enough.

THE RAY WAS A FAR LARGER CARVING than his others, simpler and more subtle. Its beauty depended not on fanciful detail but the perfect honing of the huge delta wings. Tuelen sat again in the workshop behind the shack, Villi beside him, his old eyes shining with anticipation. Tuelen had begun an hour ago and now most of the village was crowded around the open walls, watching the spectacle. The ray took shape quickly, and the wood grains flared smoothly into graceful curves. But for the first time Tuelen could feel his hands working, the tension in his fingers as they gripped the chisel, the smooth lick of the shavings as they curled back from the blade. Slowly, almost unconsciously, he began to test the force gripping him. He stilled his hand for a moment, then released it, watched the chisel resume its course. His meddling grew until finally, he began stealing control.

Villi watched this battle with interest. One moment Tuelen was shaving long swathes from a wing, and then suddenly his hand grew timid, his strokes shorter, uncertain. These fits were brief, but they left their mark. The sun was lighting the tops of the mountains when Tuelen dropped the sandpaper and sat back.

"It's beautiful," his father said huskily, hand smoothing one wing.

"But not perfect," whispered Tuelen. He knew this. He knew without looking. His hands ached, tension knotting ligaments.

"You are too hard on yourself."

Tuelen raised his eyes, and his face wore the smile of an old, old man.

"It's the strangest thing, Father. Never have I tried so hard, and it is my first real failure."

Tuelen did not go to sea the next day, or the day after that. He sat in his room with the manta before him as though praying to an effigy. But he was not praying. His eyes worked over the simple form, and the longer he looked the more obvious its imperfections became. No, *his* imperfections, Tuelen reminded himself bitterly. What a thing it would have been had he not interfered. But he had, and what was more he was *glad* of it! At least he could take credit this time, if only for imbalances.

Two nights later, the taxi arrived. The four men were sailors, but not the trawler or cargo-ship kind. With their polo shirts and self-important bearing, they could have been on holiday from a country club. They combed the village swiftly, compared workmanship and price, their speech sown with humour only they could grasp. But there was one among them more determined than the rest. His eyes were red-rimmed and glassy, swivelling warily as though certain what he sought lay hidden.

"Do you have anything bigger?" he demanded. "I need a gift for someone."

"Come with me," said Villi. When the stranger's gaze fell on the manta, Tuelen shivered: there was something indecent about the way his eyes widened. The man hefted the carving by head and tail, admired the graceful curves of the grain, the supple sweep of the wings flaring for their next powerful stroke. He conferred quietly with a companion, then turned back to Villi.

"How much, then?"

"Three hundred fifty," said Villi.

"Oh come, now. Two hundred."

"Three hundred dollars."

"I want you to carve a cribbage board into its back."

"What?"

"I'll pay two twenty-five."

"Cribbage board?" said Villi.

"Four rows of twenty holes each. Like this. And four pegs."

"Two hundred fifty dollars."

"Deal. Here's a hundred-dollar deposit. I'll be back tomorrow." And with that, the man wheeled and led his crew swiftly back to the taxi. Villi waited for the car to pull away, then turned gleefully to his son.

"*Two hundred fifty dollars!*"

Tuelen went inside and lay down on his mattress. He did not fall asleep for a long time.

The next morning, Villi waited in the workshop, the carving in his lap, drill points already marked in pencil across its back. Tuelen entered and sat on the wooden bench. Gripped in Villi's two hands the ray looked trapped, its smooth motion stilled.

"I won't do it, Father. I'm sorry."

Tuelen took a breath, braced. He had expected a slap, a scream, anything but the sad smile that spread slowly over Villi's face.

"But you already have, son. I watched you. So finish what you started. For your family. It's only wood now."

The drill belonged to Tuelen's uncle. Its worn steel housing gleamed with a dull sheen. As its bit wormed into the ray's back, Tuelen felt little but the motor's electric churn.

TUELEN WAS NOT IN BED or the workshop when Villi returned from town. Sitting at his bench, Villi hefted the small leather pouch of herbs the doctor had sold him. He was unsure whether to sneak them into Tuelen's food, or just command the boy to eat them. After the ray was sold, Tuelen had become increasingly docile. He ate little, spoke even less, and no matter how many hours he spent in bed, the bags under his eyes grew larger. That the boy would not carve annoyed Villi; what had him truly worried was his son's withdrawal from the sea. He could not recall when Tuelen had last taken the boat out. When he noticed the red gas tank gone, he assumed one of the other boys had gone fishing.

The sun had reached its apex as Tuelen gunned the outboard toward open sea. Snaking between coral heads, the water was clear and calm and blue beyond the red-brown gates of the pass. Tuelen barely looked at his lineups. Weeks had passed since he had been on the water, but he followed this path each time he closed his eyes to sleep. How many nights had the ray haunted his dreams, ghostly beautiful, arcing overhead so the sun shone through those neat rows of holes?

He killed the engine and donned his diving mask. The water felt cool as he duck-dove, kicked deeper. He recognized resident fishes, the schools of mackerel, the stripers and trevally he had watched grow, but they brought him no joy. He had felt a part of this once, then suddenly he was lost, as foreign as air to their world. Too early his lungs heaved, forced him upward, but ascending he knew the surface was no place for him either.

A few deep breaths, then he dove again. The reef reared above as he sank, deep, deeper still. For a moment Tuelen was sure the doorway was gone, but then he saw the two long fingers of trumpet coral, the huge sea fan beckoning in the current. He kicked hard, arrowing down until he was level. *This time I will pass through*, he vowed. But mere feet away he realized he could not see beyond. His head throbbed, his lungs fought to breathe. The water above squeezed him tightly, and in that moment Tuelen was afraid. He kicked violently upward, feet churning as the doorway faded behind. The pressure change cracked in his ears, his skull; the air in his lungs was empty, and the surface still so far above. *Perhaps this is where I belong*, he thought, kicking weakly. *Neither deep nor dry*. When Tuelen broke surface, he was too weak to move. He lay there gasping, drowning in air.

INSIDE PASSAGE

TED PHONED ABOUT A TOW DOWN FROM JERVIS: A construction barge, two days there and back.

"I want you on this with Drew and Robbie."

"Who's deckhand?"

"I've got some new meat. And don't twist your knickers; he's a college boy like you."

Ted had the summer habit of hiring students, then firing them when they demanded raises. Besides the cheap labour, Ken reckoned he liked breaking them on his personal wheel.

"You'll go to hell, Ted, you keep exploiting idealists."

"Fuck you, Communist. Three o'clock." And he hung up.

That was last night. Carey was at her sister's visiting the baby, so Ken phoned and they met at Riptide's for dinner. Later they'd gone to his place and had a fine time until he pulled out then what felt like her hand turned out not to be. Now the sky was heavy with cloud as he steered his truck into the puddled ruin of the parking lot. The dock felt slick underfoot as the rain began again, a cold mean drizzle. He found Drew sorting lines on *Rasputin*'s afterdeck.

"How's everything?"

"Cable's good. Robbie's checking the engine now."

Drew was a study in severity. Around deep-set eyes, the skin of his face was so tight Ken could count tendons when he talked. Ted had hired both of them the same week, but only Ken passed his skipper's exam.

"The deckie here yet?"

"Below stowing his shit. Gear bag's bigger than he is."

Drew's eyes flickered over Ken's own bag, but Ken ignored this and gazed past the tug's superstructure.

"You check the lights?"

"Worked fine yesterday."

"Well, check them again. And stow my gear, would you? I've got to look in on Rob."

"Ted wants to see you before we go so you better."

Ken paused, then continued into the depths of the ship.

Below deck was a confusion of oil and diesel fumes, the scent of metal and rain and wet rope. Ken poked his head into the engine room to find Rob spinning the coolant cap onto the Lugger's dirty bulk.

"All good?"

Rob nodded. He was a bear of a man and a fine mechanic, but not much given to elaboration. The last time they'd worked together Ken had misjudged the current under Second Narrows Bridge. One minute all was fine, then Rob brushed him aside, diesel screaming as he gunned it. Their tow missed the bridge by inches. Ever since, Ken had braced himself for demotion but heard nothing, from Ted or anyone else. Part of him longed to ask Rob why, but his larger, cowardly part seemed content with purgatory.

Drew was scribbling in the logbook as they entered the wheelhouse. Ken busied himself with charts while Rob lit the glow plugs and flicked the ignition. A few cavernous churns, then the engine settled into the cycling throb they would hear for the next two solid days.

Ken glanced at his watch. "Where's the deckie?"

"Here."

He was young with dark hair and Lennon glasses set on a fine nose. Besides the bright-blue deck boots, he wore red yacht-racing pants and a Newfoundland wool sweater below—of all things—a Greek captain's hat.

Drew recovered first.

"My *Christ*. Where's the cob pipe, Ahab?"

The slightest hesitation, then he tilted the cap over one eye and winked.

"C'mon lads, at least I look the part. This belong to someone?" He slid Ken's bag through the hatch with his foot.

Ken shot a hard look at Drew, who looked right back at him.

"Get ashore there and cast off."

"You talk to Ted?"

"What did I just say?"

Ken watched him in the side-view mirror and once the lines were free let off a blast of the foghorn and steered them smoothly from the wharf. Their VHF crackled instantly.

"*Rasputin, Rasputin.* Base."

"Yeah, Ted. Go one nine. Over." Ken keyed in the channel as Drew re-entered the wheelhouse.

"Ken, that you?"

"Roger that."

"I wanted to talk before you left. Didn't Drew mention it?"

Ken pictured Ted sitting in his cramped office, double chin on chest like a fat pink scarf. He was a short, dapper little fuck who for some reason wore blazers around the docks.

"Must have slipped his mind, boss. What's up?"

"Forget it. How are things with Paul?"

He gave the kid a slow look from head to toe.

"Just dandy."

THEY SKIRTED CAPE MUDGE and turned southeast across the Georgia Strait. There was little current and the rain had quit, sun shafts beaming down like mercy. Drew sat near Ken in the pilot's chair, cigarette lit, *Vancouver Sun* splayed across his lap. The urge to hit him was so strong Ken's hand was actually tingling, but he had seen Drew fight. Instead, he flipped radio channels and listened to the weather. When Rob and Paul appeared with mugs of coffee, Ken switched back to 16.

"How long's the run?" Paul asked, scanning the chart.

"Ninety miles. You work tugs before?"

"Yachts. The last two summers." He was in his third year at school, and when Ken asked what major, he said women's studies.

Drew's paper collapsed.

"You some kind of fag or what?"

"Why, you see something you like?"

"Nope, nothing at all."

Ken pulled out the logbook. "Paul, come here and sign this. Sit down, Drew."

The wheelhouse was cramped and smoky-warm. As Rob

shared out the last from the coffee pot, Ken saw Paul dab at his sailing pants, stained already with grease.

"There's some slicks down in the cabin. Robbie, why don't you show him where they're at."

Drew grinned wolfishly. "Watch yourself, laddie. Rob usually waits till open sea to sample the goods, but you look so fresh he might not be able to contain himself."

"You speaking from experience?"

"Sorry, friend, me and Rob are cousins."

"Never stopped your folks." He ducked as a cigarette exploded against the hatch behind him.

Drew was still scowling when Ken turned to face him. He winged open his paper with a snap.

"Don't even fucking *say* it."

Outside, there was little wind and only a two-foot swell for *Rasputin* to shove through. The jury was still out on what was worse luck: giving a ship a guy's name or changing one once it had been given, but Ken reckoned there was something right about tugs being male. Whether he should be commanding one was another question entirely.

He pulled out his phone and dialled, the air cool on his hands.

"Hello?"

"Hey, it's me. I called earlier but your phone must have been off."

"Sorry. Have you left yet?"

"Just got going."

"Oh. Well, be careful?"

"Thanks. So how's your day been?"

"Pretty good. I made a few sales?"

Carey framed all speech as questions, as though life were one long game of *Jeopardy*.

"Good. Listen, I was wondering how it went at the clinic."

"I haven't gone yet. I'm waiting until after work?"

"Oh, okay. Well, let me know what happens."

"I will. Listen, we're kind of busy?"

"Right. Okay, bye."

He hung up trying to recall a time when Carey's store had ever been busy.

They had met last fall at a house party. Ken found her sexy in a thin, frantic sort of way; she liked his face and that he would soon be a skipper. When he woke up in her bed there was snow in the valley and he stayed for breakfast. They went out for drinks days later and she wore a skirt and too much eye shadow but he appreciated the effort. She said she sold car stereos and could get him a deal if he wanted. He said maybe for the boat he was saving for: did they stock anything waterproof? There was not much else to talk about, so when they got to his place he spread his atlas on the bed and pointed out the islands he would explore in the Pacific. "I can't believe how small Tahiti is," she said, then pushed the book aside. Both felt lucky to have found someone for the winter, but winter was over.

THREE HOURS LATER Carey still had not called, and Drew would not shut up about Paul.

"You should see the crap he brought with him: computer chessboard, poetry books, even a fucking *flute!*"

It was a recorder, actually. Ken had just begun his watch when Drew entered the wheelhouse with it jutting from his mouth. A merry wink, then he aimed the tube through the hatch and issued a high, ululating squawk. Paul was at the doorway in seconds.

"How'd I sound, Zamfir?"

"If you needed something to blow on, all you had to do was ask."

Drew tossed him the instrument. "*Feltcher.*"

Paul gave it a contemplative look.

"Sure hope you rinsed this first. You never know *where* it's been."

Ken's laughter trailed Paul through the companionway. When Drew stormed outside, he laughed even harder.

Past *Rasputin*'s windows the sky was dark as a recorded female voice told Ken the person he was calling was off-air or temporarily out of range. He wondered what this woman looked like. Four months with Carey, but sometimes he could not place her voice when she phoned. They were twelve miles up the inlet, and though surrounding mountains were night-covered Ken could feel their weight pressing in. His captaincy was new enough that he still cared about protocol, so when Rob relieved him an hour later he noted weather and barometric pressure in the proper columns. The one labelled "Crew comments" he left blank.

The sleeping quarters were a cramped rectangle with two bunks pushed against opposing bulkheads. Paul lay fetal on the bottom of one, Drew on top of the other. The end of a large pack stuck out from under Paul's bed, a novel splayed on the floor near his head. Without his glasses, he looked like an entirely different person. Ken listened to their breathing blend with the rhythmic thrum of the pistons, then turned and slipped into the galley. He put the coffee on and stepped outside, tasting the heavy air, its damp salt tang. The wind had died completely, and after a few minutes he went back in, rinsed a mug with his fingers, then filled and carried it into the cabin.

Even unconscious, Drew's eyelids squeezed tighter than they should have. Ken had seen him relaxed only once—during their skipper's exam. Part of it required in-pool drills wearing exposure suits. Ken could not swim but told no one, trusting the thick neoprene to keep him up. He'd passed without incident and was feeling smug when Drew leaped with spread arms from the high-dive platform. He plunged like Icarus without the wax, then swam a breathless length, so sleek and otter-lithe that Ken had had to look away.

He placed a hand on Drew's shoulder, shook him lightly. It took another, firmer shake before he opened his eyes.

"What?"

"You're on grub detail. Here." He wafted coffee steam under Drew's nose.

"Little fag's done fuck all. Wake *him* up."

Ken took a breath, let it out slowly.

"Don't be a hard-ass; everybody takes a turn."

"Except you."

Drew rolled toward the wall and Ken measured the distance from steaming mug to exposed ear. *He'd sue,* was all he could think. Fucking Ted would represent him.

His joints felt rusted as he stole back to the galley. The smell of stew mixed with coffee as he cranked an opener around the first can. He watched the tendons of his wrist tighten, relax, tighten again until a soft sound made him turn.

Paul stood in the doorway wearing boat pants and sweater, tousled hair pushed under an Oakland As cap. There was sleep in his eyes as he stepped forward and took the opener away.

"Let me."

Ken sat and lit a cigarette as Paul unhooked a pot hanging over the range.

"Drew always been like that?"

"Yeah, but not this bad. You seem to have a talent for pissing him off."

The stew slid from the can with a splat. "Are he and Rob really cousins?"

"The original George and Lennie."

"Something should be done about him."

Paul turned and Ken studied him carefully: the green irises, the beauty mark on his cheek. Were they still called beauty marks on guys? He wasn't sure.

"This ain't college, Paul. Drew may be dumb as a box of shit but I don't need a pissing match mid-passage. Just steer clear of him. I'll speak to Ted when we get back."

Paul lit the stove with Ken's lighter and gave the pot a stir.

"Ted's my uncle, you know."

"No, I didn't know that."

"You like working for him?"

"He's tough but fair."

The kid smirked. "He's an asshole. It was his idea to get me out here. Make a *man* out of me."

"Well, I guess everyone's related to someone."

Paul went on with his stirring.

NO BORDER BETWE‾N SLEEP AND WAKING, just a slow swim upward, their voices the surface after a long time under.

". . . looking at me like that."

"Like what?"

"And writing in that book of yours. Keep that up and I'm coming over there."

Ken's eyes opened to a smear of light. He touched the humming wall to orient himself.

"I'll read it if you'd like."

"I don't even want to fucking *know*."

"But it's just your style. *His sort of man is new to me, salt-licked, with a leathered roughness replacing what he might say had he felt the need.*"

Ken made out two legs hanging from the bunk above, and beyond them, Paul sprawled on his own, notebook in hand.

"*One almost envies a woman's chance to learn that soul through skin, to feel weathered hide against your cheek as you seek the cracks to let you see . . .*"

A flicker as Drew launched forward.

The night they wrote their skipper's exams, Carey met Ken's class at Riptide's. Despite their best efforts, Drew was in a foul mood. He knew he'd flunked the Colregs, and when some jock with football-pad shoulders spilled beer down his shirt he snapped. Ken watched Drew's fist drive into the footballer's throat, his bent knee rise viciously for the groin. But what he recalled most clearly was Carey beside him, lips parted, her brown eyes tracking each blow. Drew's rage was less savage. He'd moved too fast for the man, for any of them; he would kill Paul if he could. Ken sprang up, head cracking the bed frame, but worse was the seized zipper of his sleeping bag.

This is how Rob found them: Drew atop Paul in one corner,

and Ken pinned in his bunk like a papoose. A moment's pause, then Rob plucked Drew off by his collar.

"Quit," Rob said, and shook him a little.

Paul was still crouched in the corner when Ken finally worked himself free. There was a welt under one eye, and his upper lip swelled as Ken watched, but otherwise he looked all right. Rob pushed Drew out of the cabin to cool down, then turned back to his captain. Ken meant to thank him, but all he said was: "Why aren't you on watch?"

The big man shrugged. "I was coming to get you. We're nearly there."

SUNRISE WAS AN HOUR OLD but aside from a muted glow through cloud there was little light to speak of. Ken watched bolts of fog drape Jervis's near shores and flipped the VHF to the weather station. After a minute of nothing but fog warnings he switched it off, lit a cigarette, and listened to *Rasputin*'s own brand of quiet. He tried not to think about Drew, or the kid, or Carey having one of his. When Rob appeared with yet another pot of coffee, Ken asked him to send Paul up.

His eye had swelled shut but the kid still managed a smile as he slumped in the navigator's chair.

"Pen mightier than the sword, my *ass*."

Ken harnessed his grin.

"I asked Rob to get you because I want you to know what's happening. It's a construction barge we're towing, a pretty big one. Got a crane and a dozer and crew quarters. Anyway, I normally wouldn't bother, but there's a lot of fog so I want you to man the barge horn."

"Fine."

"Good. So get some gear together and be ready to go."

Malibu was a frontier-styled resort town built at the mouth of Princess Louisa Inlet. Radar found the tow before Ken did, and as it loomed out of the fog he brought *Rasputin* stern-to under a rung ladder near the bow. The barge was old, with flaking paint, and lay in deep water on a mooring. Drew and Paul set their lines. Ken left the wheelhouse and followed them up the ladder.

"Drew, help Rob hook up the cable. Paul, you're with me."

A one-axle, one-window construction trailer sat on blocks near the stern of the barge. Behind it crouched a Honda generator and, as Ken cracked the fuel tank, Paul searched and found some red plastic cans of unleaded. On the third pull the generator coughed to life and Ken entered the trailer, hit the lights. The air smelled of coffee and cigarettes and men. He leaned down and turned on a dusty block heater lying by a military cot. Its thin mattress was bare and Ken noticed but did not mention the mouse scat on the floor underneath. Soon the heater's coils glowed red and Ken left it on "medium," then went back outside with Paul following. The foghorn was farthest aft, and after a test Ken explained the controls. The generator's mutterings ruined the silence, but the air's woolly dampness gave Ken the feeling that he was hearing the day through a pillow.

"What's the score?" he asked his mate at the bow.

"We're loose." Drew slid fireman-style down the ladder. Paul made to follow but Ken held him back, passed him a coil of light line he'd brought.

"I'll send your stuff up with this. Where is it?"

Paul studied him a moment. "My bunk."

"You'll be fine," Ken said, then started down.

The crew quarters still smelled of sleep. Paul's bag was there, but only later would Ken recall the sheaf of paper atop Drew's worn pillow.

The fog thickened as Paul hauled his gear up the messenger. Drew waved after it, wide grin on his hatchet face.

"Play safe, shit-beard!"

Ken poked his head out of the pilot house and waved himself. When Paul's eye met his, damned if he didn't wink right at him.

The diesel's pitch dropped as *Rasputin* leaned into the load. Drew slipped below, and Ken was about to have Rob give the tow more leash when his phone made a digital bleat.

"Hello?"

"Hi, it's me?"

Ken smiled. "Hello, me. How are you?"

"Fine. Everything's fine here?"

"That's great. I know those day-after pills are rough on your system but—"

"Yeah, listen: Greg gave me tomorrow off so I'm heading down to Victoria for the weekend? I'm leaving my phone but didn't want you to worry?"

Ken stepped toward the hatch. "Did something happen? Did they give you a hard time?"

"No, they were really nice. I talked with the nurse for like two hours."

"Really. About what?"

"Oh, everything. Life. Options?"

"But she gave you the pill, right?"

"Not exactly? Look, I've got to go."

Rather than smash his phone through the window, Ken took a slow breath.

"Carey, tell me what happened."

She had just briefed him on probabilities and not living with guilt when Ken heard a different sound over the humming engine. He stepped out on deck to find Drew as far aft as he could get, screaming. He was cursing and waved the same paper Ken had seen on his pillow, and forty yards behind, Paul stood where he had waited on the lip of the barge's bow.

"Faggot motherfucker! You're fucking dead, you hear me?! Dead! You want to fuck me?! I'll cut off your cock and choke you with it!"

As Ken watched, Paul cupped a hand to his ear. His smile was wide and triumphant and looked as if nothing could wipe it off, but the tow kept drifting to port. When the bridle snapped the bow in line, Paul's smile slipped and he fell and the barge stepped on his splash like a foot on a cigarette.

"—I won't kill it, Ken. And like she said: Fate makes no mistakes. Honey? Are you there?"

"I have to go now," he said, meek.

Math was not his strong suit, but in the time Ken took to reach the wheel he figured the 150-foot barge would take twenty seconds to clear Paul's head, twenty black, panicked seconds of bouncing off a barnacled hull. He rammed the throttle as far as it would go, their bow lifting, but water moved faster than weight and the prop-wash astern was what he wanted. After a ten count, he killed the engine, cut the wheel to starboard and raced aft. Rob had already hoisted the dinghy, and with Ken guiding it over the port rail jumped in and fired the engine. Ken leaped in after him.

The inflatable was soft and cold spray cut them as they charged toward the oil-flat wake of the barge. Ken did not know how long Paul had been down but knew any time was too long in forty-degree water.

"There." Rob changed course and dropped the dinghy off its plane.

Paul looked bad. Blood streamed from his head and hands but he was still breathing when they pulled him aboard. As they roared back to *Rasputin*, Drew stepped from the bridge and Ken slung him the painter as Rob lifted Paul out. By the time they reached the wheelhouse he was unconscious; it wasn't the corpse-cold skin that worried Ken, but the fact that Paul had stopped shivering.

"Get his clothes off! Drew, get the sleeping bags up here!"

Rob stripped Paul down as Ken made his mayday call. His hands and voice shook with cold as he reported their situation to the Coast Guard. Thirty minutes to scramble a chopper, they said. Behind him, Drew appeared at the door with their sleeping bags. Ken stooped, called Paul's name; nothing. Drew laid another sleeping bag over him, but all the insulation in the world meant fuck all if the kid had no heat.

"The dumb cunt."

Ken glanced up. Drew looked more angry than scared, but warm and dry.

"Get your clothes off."

"What?"

"I said get your kit off. Now."

"What for?"

"We've got to warm him up. You're getting in there."

"Like hell. Put Rob in."

"Rob's as cold as I am. Get 'em off. That's an order."

Drew grinned. "Since you put it that way, Skipper, *fuck you*."

Ken stood slowly. "Listen, you son of a bitch: if you don't get in there he could die!"

"But the *blood*."

His voice was impossibly soft but his fear was real and so wrong that Ken's knees buckled under the weight of it.

"Please, will someone *once* just do what I say?"

Drew's mouth twitched, his "no" building when Rob's fist caught him up and forward of the ear. He rocked back and would have fallen if not for the chart table. Grabbing his shirt, Rob tore downward. Another tug and it was off. Drew's chest was narrow and white, nipples ringed by light blond hairs. He stood quaking as Rob unlaced his boots.

"Wait," Ken said.

His fingers were stupid with cold, shirt buttons hard as teeth between them. His pants came off more easily, belt striking the steel floor with a clang. Beneath the blankets, Paul's skin was marble smooth, his wet hair reeking of mammal and sea, and Ken cradled him like a man drowning.

ACKNOWLEDGEMENTS

THESE STORIES ARE WORKS OF FICTION. THE TRAVELS encompassing them were furthered by many. Thanks to George Jeffords, George von Angel, Kathy Fisher, Susan Brown, Bev Armstrong (the most accommodating of travel agents), Hapi, Akim, Chris Patterson, Carol and Bill Lawler and the whole *Wendy Lynne* family. Also thanks to Jerry Aherne, who opened my door to Vancouver, and the '99 PRISM Board, who gave me reason to stay. For their input and emotional support, thanks to Peter Oliva, Rachel Wyatt, Edna Alford, Dianne Warren, Joan Skogan and Guy Vanderhaeghe. Financial aid from the Alberta Foundation for the Arts, the Canada Council and the Banff Centre is greatly appreciated. Special thanks to my editor, Barbara Berson, for taking a risk, and to my agent, Denise Bukowski, for working so hard for one. Thanks to Cheryl Cohen for her copy-editing expertise.

And a final thank you to Captain Drew Peerless, who taught me all I know about sailing and absolutely nothing about women.